THE CALL TO
VENGEANCE

Before there was the Phantom Menace, there was . . .

JEDI APPRENTICE

. . . and more to come

JEDI APPRENTICE SPECIAL EDITION
#1 Deceptions

JEDI APPRENTICE

The Call to Vengeance

Jude Watson

LUCAS BOOKS

SCHOLASTIC INC.

New York Toronto London Auckland Sydney
Mexico City New Delhi Hong Kong Buenos Aires

ISBN 0-439-13935-X

Cover art by Cliff Nielsen.

12 11 10 9 8 7 6 5 4 3 2 1   1 2 3 4 5 6/0

Printed in the U.S.A.
First Scholastic printing, December 2001

THE CALL TO VENGEANCE

CHAPTER 1

The light tubes in the large dwelling were powered down to half strength and set to a faint blue hue. The hallways were hushed and dim. Beyond a pair of opaque glass double doors, a single glass column stood, as tall as a human figure. It gave off a soft, steady glow.

Blue was the color of mourning on the planet of New Apsolon. Glass columns were used to commemorate those who had lost their lives to injustice. This slender shaft of pure light was for the Jedi Knight Tahl.

Manex, the brother of Roan, the late ruler of New Apsolon, had offered the Jedi his own home in which to mourn Tahl. Manex had tried to save Tahl by summoning the best med team in New Apsolon to treat her. When she had died, he had made the appropriate arrangements. He himself had gone to find the column of light to mark her spirit.

Obi-Wan Kenobi struggled to feel grateful. He did not trust Manex. He did not trust the man's great wealth or his character. Manex was not interested in anyone's well-being but his own. Why was he being so kind to the Jedi?

Obi-Wan wished he could talk to his Master about it. But Qui-Gon Jinn was unreachable. He had gone inside the room with Tahl and had remained there ever since.

Obi-Wan sat on the floor outside. He had begun by standing, but exhaustion finally forced him to sit. He wanted to lie down, but he would remain upright as long as he could. It was the only thing he could think of to do for his Master.

The shock was wearing off, but Obi-Wan still had difficulty understanding that Tahl was gone. It meant looking ahead to a future that did not hold her spirit, her humor, and her fierce intelligence. There had been so many times that a kind word or a quick smile had restored him. Tahl knew his Master, Qui-Gon Jinn, better than anyone else. She had helped Obi-Wan to understand Qui-Gon. Obi-Wan even suspected that she had played a role in bringing the two of them together after he had left the Jedi order. That had been a deep rift, hard to heal. Yet Obi-

Wan had always taken great comfort from the feeling that Tahl wanted Qui-Gon to take him back. She had comprehended more clearly than anyone why he had done what he did. She knew he had truly learned an important lesson about his own character, and she wanted Qui-Gon to give him a second chance.

He had learned many things as a Jedi student — how to turn fear into purpose, how to deepen discipline into will. But how could he turn grief into acceptance? There could be no acceptance of this. Yet somehow he must keep going until he found it.

At first he had been filled with such pain that he could hardly think. Tahl had been kidnapped by Balog, the Chief Security Controller of the planet. He had drugged her and imprisoned her in a sensory deprivation device used for torturing political prisoners. She had been weak when they had released her. But Obi-Wan had felt certain that Tahl's great strength combined with her Jedi powers would save her. Never for one second had he considered the possibility that she would die.

Neither, he was sure, had his Master. When he had run into Tahl's room at the med center, he had seen Qui-Gon bent over Tahl's still body. He saw the sensors stream by in flat, crisp lines, showing that her vital signs were gone. Still Qui-Gon did not move. He held Tahl's hand and pressed his forehead against hers. Obi-Wan had not only seen his grief, he had felt it like a living shadow in the room. He realized at that moment that Qui-Gon's feelings for Tahl were deeper than friendship. They were as deep and complex as the man himself. Qui-Gon had loved her.

There was nothing Obi-Wan could do to help his Master now. Qui-Gon had not responded to his words or his presence. Obi-Wan desperately wished he were older than sixteen. Maybe with more maturity he would know how to comfort someone whose world had collapsed.

It hurt him to see Qui-Gon suffering. His Master had only left Tahl's room once, to rush out on a mysterious errand. He had tersely told Obi-Wan when he returned that he had managed to find two more probe droids. He had sent them to track down Balog. Now he would return to Tahl's side.

"Is there anything I can do, Master?" Obi-Wan had asked.

"Nothing," Qui-Gon had replied, and closed the door behind him.

Obi-Wan was used to silence between them.

It was often a form of communication. He had come to understand that his Master was a man of few words. But this silence was different. He could not read it. Over and over the words Qui-Gon had spoken at Tahl's deathbed ran in his head: *There is no help for me now. There is only revenge.*

Revenge. Obi-Wan had never heard Qui-Gon use that word. It was not a concept the Jedi would ever endorse. *No revenge, only justice.* That creed was written on the heart of every Jedi. Revenge led to the dark side. It twisted the mind and crippled duty into something full of ego and darkness.

Was Qui-Gon battling the dark side inside himself? Balog had taken away what was most dear to him. He had done it in the most cruel way imaginable. He had drained Tahl minute by minute of her strength.

Had Qui-Gon sent out the probe droids in order to find Balog so that he could kill him?

Obi-Wan pushed the thought away. He had to trust his Master. Qui-Gon would find the calm center he needed to proceed. They must find Balog, but in the interest of justice, not revenge.

If a Jedi died during a mission, the Jedi Council was supposed to be contacted immediately. Obi-Wan, in the first period of deep shock after Tahl's death, had roused himself to ask Qui-Gon about this. Qui-Gon had not answered. Obi-Wan could see how little procedure meant to Qui-Gon now. So the apprentice had been the one to contact the Jedi Council and inform them what had happened.

Yoda had been shocked and deeply distressed, for he had cared about Tahl, too. A Jedi team would be sent immediately. Over the course of the day, Obi-Wan had wondered who it would be. If they had left immediately and taken a fast ship, it wouldn't be long until they reached New Apsolon. He wasn't sure how he felt about that. A Jedi team would be reassuring . . . but would they notice that Qui-Gon was not acting like himself?

Manex appeared in the hall, and Obi-Wan scrambled to his feet.

"Has he come out?" Manex asked, his plump face creased in worry.

"Not for hours," Obi-Wan replied.

"Please let me know if I can be of service. I must go to the United Legislature. They've called for me. Things are very unsettled in the government right now. I will be back as soon as I can. I've given instructions to security to show your Jedi team in as soon as they arrive."

"Thank you," Obi-Wan said.

Qui-Gon stepped into the hall seconds after Manex left.

"I heard voices," he said heavily.

"Manex has gone to the United Legislature," Obi-Wan said. "Is there anything I can get you, Master?"

"No. Have the probe droids returned?"

Obi-Wan shook his head. "I'll notify you as soon as they do, of course. But I think there are other things we can do to capture Balog, Master. We don't have to wait for the probe droids." He spoke hurriedly, before Qui-Gon could turn away and go back inside the room. During the long wait, Obi-Wan had been thinking about their next step. It was the only thing that pushed away the pain.

"Eritha is still staying with Alani in the Supreme Governor's Residence," he went on. "She is concealing the fact that she knows her sister is in league with the Absolutes, hoping to gain more information. She promised to be a spy for us. Alani might know where Balog is."

"So we must wait for that, too," Qui-Gon said.

"But we could investigate the tie between them," Obi-Wan pointed out. "How was the alliance formed? What does Alani expect from

Balog? What does he want in return? Where did the Absolutes retreat to after their base was destroyed in the quarries? And what about the list of the Absolutes' secret informers? Balog doesn't have it, because he's looking for it. We know that the Worker Oleg might have had it before he disappeared." Obi-Wan swallowed. Qui-Gon's gaze went dim. The reason they knew that was because Tahl had told them. He pushed on.

"If we can find the list first, we can set a trap for Balog. And what about Manex? What reason does he have for being so kind to us? There are many leads to investigate. I'm sure there must be rumors swirling at the United Legislature. Some of them should be followed up on —"

"We are here to find Tahl's killer, not get involved in politics," Qui-Gon said sternly. "Our main object is the pursuit of Balog. As soon as we get information on him, I can leave."

"You mean *we* can leave," Obi-Wan amended, watching his Master carefully.

Neither one of them had heard the footsteps approaching.

"We came as soon as we could," a deep familiar voice said.

Obi-Wan turned. The Jedi team had arrived. To his relief, he saw his good friend Bant. But his relief turned to disquiet when he saw the Jedi Master was next to her. It was Mace Windu.

CHAPTER 2

Mace Windu took only the most crucial missions now. His duties on the Jedi Council were many. Obi-Wan realized more fully how important the loss of Tahl was to the Jedi. He had been thinking of himself and Qui-Gon only, of the friend they had lost. But Tahl's influence ran much deeper and wider.

Mace gave both Qui-Gon and Obi-Wan a long, measured look. He seemed to capture their weariness and grief as well as the tension between them. Obi-Wan wondered how much of their discussion Mace had heard. He grew uncomfortable under that all-seeing glance.

He turned with relief to his friend Bant. They had gone through Temple training together, and she was the being he most relied on for her support and understanding. But there was something cool in the way Bant returned his regard. Obviously, she was upset. She had been Tahl's apprentice.

"We are sorry to be here under such tragic circumstances," Bant said to Qui-Gon.

Obi-Wan even picked up a hint of coolness in her greeting to Qui-Gon. That was a bigger surprise. Bant revered Qui-Gon, and Qui-Gon had a special place in his heart for Obi-Wan's friend.

Qui-Gon did not seem to notice the change. He was too consumed by his own grief, Obi-Wan knew. He nodded at Bant.

"Tahl is inside," he said.

"We will see her for a moment," Mace said. "Then I would like a briefing on where we stand."

Qui-Gon gave a heavy nod. Mace and Bant disappeared inside. They returned after a few minutes. Bant looked shaken. Mace closed the double doors behind them quietly and moved farther down the hall.

"This Chief Security Controller, Balog, was responsible," Mace said. "We know this for sure, yet we don't know where he is. Correct?"

Qui-Gon did not speak, so Obi-Wan said, "Yes."

"Tell me what happened," Mace said, his

eyes on Obi-Wan. He seemed to understand that Qui-Gon did not want to talk. Qui-Gon's eyes were on the door to the room where Tahl was, as though only the slimmest whisper of respect was keeping him in the hall.

"Once we knew that Balog had captured Tahl, we obtained two probe droids to track him," Obi-Wan explained.

Mace frowned. "Aren't probe droids now illegal on this planet?"

"Yes," Obi-Wan said, swallowing. He was well aware that Jedi were not supposed to break laws on other worlds. "But you can buy them on the black market. It was our only chance to find Tahl. We had good reason to believe she would be in a sensory deprivation device, so we knew that the longer it took to find her, the more danger she would be in. The probe droids told us that Balog had struck out across open country and entered the quarry region of the planet. Eritha, one of the daughters of the late ruler, Ewane, followed us. She had discovered that her twin sister, Alani, was in league with the Absolutes. This was a shock, because both Eritha and Alani are Workers. When the Civilized were in power, they used the Absolutes for surveillance and torture of Workers — including Alani and Eritha's father."

"I know the Absolutes were the secret police of New Apsolon," Bant said hesitantly. "I didn't get a chance to be thoroughly briefed. Weren't they outlawed after Ewane was elected?"

"Yes. But the Workers suspect that the secret police never disbanded," Obi-Wan said. "We discovered that they are right. But we never suspected Balog was in league with them. He's a Worker and was a protégé of Ewane. Now we know from Eritha that Alani arranged the kidnapping of herself and her sister to throw us off the track and gain public sympathy. At the same time, we believe it was a trick to lure Roan into the hands of the Absolutes. Roan was elected after Ewane was killed."

"Roan was a Civilized, not a Worker," Bant said.

"Right. But he had great sympathy for the Worker cause and worked closely with Ewane to bring about justice for all the people of New Apsolon. He even took in the twins when Ewane was murdered."

"And Alani betrayed him," Bant said slowly. "She must be very corrupt."

"We stumbled onto a village of Rock Workers while we were pursuing Balog," Obi-Wan went on. "Their entire village was destroyed in a raid, except for one Rock Worker, Yanci. She's the one who helped us find the secret headquarters of the Absolutes. That's how we rescued Tahl. But it was too late. Qui-Gon brought her back here, but the damage to her internal organs was too severe. . . ."

"Balog killed her slowly," Qui-Gon said. His voice sounded hoarse and rusty.

"He escaped in an underwater aqua skimmer," Obi-Wan added. "He was impossible to track, and we needed to get Tahl to safety."

"And now?" Mace asked. "We see on the streets that there is unrest here. If Alani is planning some sort of takeover, it will be soon. Immediate pursuit of Balog is wise."

"That is what we think," Qui-Gon said.

"Yet attention to the mission at hand will also bring results," Mace went on. "If Balog is now in hiding, we'll need to track him by his ambitions. Ambitions reveal direction."

"The Workers contacted me," Obi-Wan said. "They investigated all the file systems in the Absolute headquarters. Everything had been wiped clean. We don't have much to go on."

"We have our instincts," Mace said. He

turned to Qui-Gon. "Is there a place we can speak alone, Qui-Gon?"

Reluctantly, Qui-Gon nodded. He turned and led the way down the hall.

As soon as they were alone, Obi-Wan turned to Bant. "I'm so sorry about Tahl," he said in a rush. "I know how you must feel —"

"I don't think so." Bant's tone was flat. She looked at him steadily with her large silver eyes. Mon Calamari had extraordinarily clear eyes, and Obi-Wan had always been able to read Bant's emotions. Now he was confused by the anger he saw there.

"Your sympathy comes too late," Bant continued. "How could you keep the fact that Tahl had been kidnapped from me, Obi-Wan? You know that you and Qui-Gon should have contacted the Temple immediately."

"I know," Obi-Wan said. "But so much happened so fast. Qui-Gon thought that more Jedi might endanger Tahl's life. We decided that if we couldn't rescue her in twenty-four hours, we would contact the Temple." Actually, it had been *Qui-Gon's* decision to wait. But Obi-Wan would take responsibility for it, too. He could have argued with Qui-Gon. He had not.

"That wasn't your decision to make," Bant interrupted. Her normally gentle voice was crisp with anger. "How would you feel if another Jedi team had done that to you, Obi-Wan? What if Qui-Gon had been kidnapped?"

Obi-Wan felt shame wash over him. Qui-Gon had been kidnapped once, by the scientist Jenna Zan Arbor. If he hadn't been involved in Qui-Gon's rescue, he would have gone crazy.

"We didn't think it through," he admitted.

"I'll say," Bant said bitterly. She had never taken such a harsh tone with him. "Did you think of me at all, Obi-Wan?"

"Of course," Obi-Wan said. "I thought I would save you a day of worry. If we couldn't rescue Tahl, we would have called in a Jedi team."

"But you didn't rescue Tahl," Bant said evenly. "At least, not in time. Did you?"

Obi-Wan was stung. Bant had said nothing more than the terrible truth, but it wasn't like her to hurt him that way.

She seemed to realize how severely her words had wounded him. "She was my Master, Obi-Wan," she said in a slightly softer tone. "She needed me. I wasn't there. You can't imagine how that feels."

"No," he said quietly. "And I never would want to. I am truly sorry, Bant. You are right. We should have contacted you."

Bant nodded stiffly. Obi-Wan's actions had caused a rift in their friendship. He didn't know how deep that rift was, or how long it would last.

Tahl was dead. Qui-Gon was like a stranger. And now Obi-Wan's best friend had turned away from him.

He had never felt so alone.

CHAPTER 3

The last thing Qui-Gon wanted was a private talk with Mace Windu. He felt such a heaviness of spirit that it was all he could do to be courteous to the Jedi Master. The pain inside him ebbed and flowed like an unpredictable tide. Sometimes it reared up so fiercely that it tore at his insides like a beast.

Out of all the Jedi, why did Mace have to take this mission? There was a great deal of respect between the two Jedi, but Qui-Gon had never felt particularly close to his formidable colleague.

The door slid shut behind them. Even here in his private reception room, Manex had turned the lights to pale blue. It gave an eerie cast to the gleaming black stone that covered the walls and floors, and turned the bright vivid greens of the seating areas and lush pillows into a sickly hue.

"Do you wish to accompany Tahl's body back to the Temple?" Mace asked. "Bant, Obi-Wan, and I can remain here and conduct the mission."

Qui-Gon saw that Mace was trying to be kind. There was deep sympathy in his sober gaze. He felt a rush of relief that Mace did not inquire into his feelings, or ask if there had been something deeper than friendship between Qui-Gon and Tahl. Qui-Gon suspected that Mace already knew these things without words.

Qui-Gon did not intend to give up the search for Tahl's killer. But he needed to be careful. He could not tell Mace that his need to find Balog was burning inside him. His anger might show in his voice or his face. Mace might think that the anger was not under control. He would not understand that despite his grief, Qui-Gon's control was complete.

It is because it has to be. It's the only way I can go on.

"Thank you for the offer," he said. "But I must continue the mission in order to honor Tahl's memory."

To Qui-Gon's relief, Mace nodded. He was not going to argue with him. Tahl would have. She always knew when he was trying to sidestep his own feelings. A fresh spurt of agony caused him to clench his hands together into fists by his side. If Mace noticed, he did not comment.

The light over the door flashed, then slid open partway. Manex's protocol droid, fashioned of highly polished black plastoid, hovered.

"Manex has returned and would like a word with the Jedi," it said.

Glad for the interruption, Qui-Gon turned. "Please tell him to come in."

A moment later the door opened wider and Manex entered, along with Obi-Wan and Bant.

"Excuse the interruption please," Manex said, running a hand through his cropped curly hair. For the first time, Qui-Gon noticed that it had begun to turn gray like his brother's. "I have just come from the United Legislature, and I have some news that I thought you needed to hear. I'm glad to see the new Jedi team has arrived."

"I am Mace Windu and this is Bant," Mace said.

Manex bowed his greeting. "I'm honored to have distinguished Jedi in my home. But I'm afraid that my news is not good. Information has been leaked to the Senators that Tahl was helping the Absolutes. There is a holotape of a meeting that she chaired in which she is discussing taking over the government."

"Tahl was working undercover in order to *expose* the Absolutes," Obi-Wan explained.

"The Senators don't know what to believe," Manex said.

"How did this tape get circulated?" Mace asked.

"Balog," Obi-Wan and Qui-Gon said together.

"Obviously it's been leaked by him," Obi-Wan continued. "He needs to discredit the Jedi in order to prepare the way to return to power."

"It doesn't matter," Qui-Gon said. "We'll clear Tahl's name when we find Balog."

"If you can find him quickly," Manex said gravely. "My fear is that he will come to·power and we won't be able to charge him with anything. Do you know who is backing him? Whoever it is, he or she must be powerful."

"We are not certain of anything," Mace said. The Jedi were not ready to confide in Manex. He knew nothing of Alani's treachery. He might even be an ally of hers.

"I have further news," Manex said. "I have been appointed Acting Supreme Governor until the elections are held. I haven't sought this position, nor do I want it. I'm a businessman, not a politician. But the Senators prevailed on my love of my planet and my desire for peace. They feel that Roan's brother has the best chance of holding the government together. No doubt the election period will be volatile. I've tightened security and closed the Absolute Museum. We are mainly trying to keep the people calm. And there's one more thing. As Acting Supreme Governor, I'm making an official request to the Jedi. I'd like you to oversee the preparations for the upcoming elections. We are holding them in three days. We can't afford to wait. It's the only way to keep the peace."

"But not everyone trusts the Jedi," Obi-Wan said. "I'm sure the Tahl holotape didn't help."

"There are enough who do," Manex said. "And once you find Balog, as you said, Tahl's name will be cleared. Until then, you'll have all my support. I've instructed World Security to give you cooperation."

Mace nodded. "Then we accept."

Qui-Gon bristled. Mace had not even glanced at him, or sought his opinion. He would have been against the acceptance.

"I'll leave you, then," Manex said. He rushed out, his gold robe swirling around his soft, polished boots.

Qui-Gon knew he should speak diplomatically, but he didn't have time for tact. "This is a mistake," he told Mace. "Overseeing elections will divert us from the investigation of Tahl's death. We should be concentrating on finding Balog."

Mace took Qui-Gon's stern tone in stride. "I disagree," he said. "The political situation is part of the pursuit of justice for Tahl's killer. It is all tied together. We will be in the perfect position to gain information. Not to mention that our overall mission was to restore New Apsolon to stability. If the Supreme Governor requests our help in a legitimate cause, the Jedi must agree."

Qui-Gon pressed his lips together. He knew better than to push the argument further. But he was furious at Mace's decision. He wanted to stalk out of the room, out of the house, and keep going. He wanted to push an airspeeder as fast as he could, even without a direction. Frustration boiled inside him. With every second that ticked away, he could feel Balog slipping out of his reach.

CHAPTER 4

"I suggest that we find our quarters and take some refreshment," Mace said, turning to Bant. "We had a long journey, and we don't know when we'll get a chance to rest. Then we'll head to the United Legislature and get started."

Obi-Wan had felt Qui-Gon's displeasure with Mace's decision. It was clear how deeply he disagreed with Mace. Obi-Wan knew that Qui-Gon saw this as a waste of time. But his Master had not come up with an alternative plan, either.

Mace lifted an eyebrow at Qui-Gon. "If you had an idea of Balog's whereabouts, or a way to find him, we would delay and follow your lead. But until then, the only course open to us is to gather information."

Obi-Wan glanced at Qui-Gon. His Master had not told Mace about the probe droids he'd sent out to find Balog. It was one thing to break the laws of a planet because a Jedi was in immediate danger of death. It was another to employ them in tracking a citizen of the planet where they were illegal. He wasn't sure how Mace would react, which was most likely why Qui-Gon did not tell him. The Jedi were already on uncertain footing on the planet.

Mace and Bant left the room. The tension did not dissolve. Qui-Gon paced, brooding. Clearly, he did not want to talk.

Manex's protocol droid once again hovered in the doorway. "So sorry to intrude. Another visitor. She says you know her, so I took the liberty. Her name is Yanci."

"Yanci? Show her in, please," Obi-Wan said, surprise in his voice. Yanci was the Rock Worker medic who had fixed his leg after a rock had crushed it. She had come after them and begged for their help in resisting an Absolute attack on their settlement. Obi-Wan and Qui-Gon had returned with her, but it was too late. Every man, woman, and child had been killed. Yanci's terrible grief still burned in Obi-Wan's memory.

Yanci entered the room. Obi-Wan could see at once that she had changed in the course of two days. The massacre of her fellow Workers along with the death of the man she loved had etched sorrow into her features. Her eyes were different. He could see the loss there.

For the first time since Tahl's death, Qui-Gon's

distraction lifted and he truly seemed to focus on another person. It was as though the two recognized each other immediately as fellow sufferers. He moved forward and took her hand. "It is good to see you," he murmured.

She stared into his face. "I heard about Jedi Knight Tahl. You have my deepest sympathy."

He pressed her hand, then dropped it. Obi-Wan saw that Qui-Gon did not need words with Yanci.

She turned to Obi-Wan. "And how is that leg?"

"All healed, thanks to you."

"And you. I have great respect for the Jedi powers of recuperation. I am sorry to come at such a time. I'm living with the Workers in the city now." Yanci's voice lowered. "I heard something that I thought might help you. It is about a Worker named Oleg."

Obi-Wan's senses sharpened. Oleg was the Worker who they believed had the list of Absolute informers. He had been seen with Tahl, which was why Balog suspected that he had passed off the list to her. Instead, he had disappeared.

"I heard that Balog is chasing Oleg," Yanci went on. "I don't know why, and I don't need to know. But I recognized that name. Several weeks ago, the Rock Workers were contacted by the Workers in the city. They asked if they could send a Worker to us who needed to go into hiding. It was Oleg. He had infiltrated the Absolutes and needed a place to hide once his mission was completed. They weren't sure when he would be coming. We agreed, of course. Later we got word that his cover had been blown and that he was being sent immediately. But he never showed up. We were concerned and searched the quarries, but we don't think he ever left the city. Then we ourselves were attacked. As you know."

"Thank you for coming to us," Qui-Gon said.

Obi-Wan could hear the disappointment in his voice. He felt disappointed as well. The information was interesting, but not very helpful. It didn't lead them any closer to Balog.

"But that is not all I have come to tell you," Yanci said. "There was a reason the Workers were sending him to us. They knew that I had training in a specific medical condition that Oleg has. He got it as a result of being imprisoned by the Absolutes years ago. It's a form of hibernation sickness that recurs regularly, requiring treatment. I happen to be able to provide treatment because several of our Rock Workers had the same syndrome. But there are only a few med clinics in the city that can treat it. So I thought . . . I thought it would be a way to track Oleg, if you were looking for him. It could be a way to find Balog."

Yanci reached inside her cloak and took out a durasheet. She handed it to Qui-Gon. "Here is a list of the clinics."

Obi-Wan felt his spirits rise. If they could track Oleg, no doubt they would find Balog. Qui-Gon appeared frozen, transfixed by the list in his hand.

"Do you think it could be helpful?" Yanci asked.

"Yes," Qui-Gon said. "Very."

Qui-Gon clutched the list, staring at it so fiercely that Yanci glanced at Obi-Wan, concerned.

Obi-Wan moved forward to thank her. "This will help us," he told Yanci. "Thank you for coming. I'll see you out."

He walked her to the front door and bid her good-bye. He hurried back down the hall to Qui-Gon, eager to discuss their next step.

But when he opened the door to the sitting room, his Master had disappeared.

CHAPTER 5

Qui-Gon knew he should not have left Manex's residence without telling Obi-Wan or Mace where he was going, but he did not regret it. More talk meant more delay. If he had taken Obi-Wan with him, he would have put his Padawan in a bad position. If Qui-Gon was going to have conflicts with Mace Windu, he did not want Obi-Wan to be involved in them.

And, truth be told, his instincts told him that he needed to do this alone. Four Jedi equaled four opinions, more talk, more discussion. He didn't have the time. If he were going to find Balog, he had to move fast.

His comlink signaled. It was the third time in an hour. He knew it was Obi-Wan. He could feel that his Padawan wanted urgently to speak with him. Qui-Gon hesitated and then shut his comlink off. He would contact Obi-Wan when he had hard information. His Padawan would understand, he hoped.

Yanci's information could be useless. It wouldn't take him long to check out four clinics. In the meantime, Mace could go to the United Legislature and talk all he wanted.

So far he had been to three clinics. Oleg was not listed on the roster of patients. Of course, Oleg could have used an assumed name, but that would be hard to do. Medical treatment was free on New Apsolon, and records were kept on all citizens who needed treatment. The records were accessed by retinal scan. When Oleg needed treatment, the clinic would need his records in order to treat him. No doubt he would have to take the chance and use his own name.

Qui-Gon approached the last clinic on the outskirts of the Civilized Sector. So far it had been easy to determine whether or not Oleg had been a patient at a clinic. Qui-Gon had been able to bluff or charm his way into getting the information out of the clerks. The clinics were not run on high security. He expected the last one to be easy as well. Soon, if he was lucky, Balog could be within his grasp. His hopes rose as he strode toward the entrance.

A woman stood outside, hesitating. Qui-Gon moved forward to open the door, then saw that she was blind. He stopped and watched as she reached out, searching for the door access panel.

How many times had Tahl snapped at him to let her do something herself? He had learned to let her pour the tea, access a datafile, lead the way to the lake.

I can't bear it when you hover, she would say. *I know I'm blind, but I still have a sense of direction.*

Even the smallest memories of Tahl brought him such great pain. Maybe the small memories were the worst. It was thousands of such small memories that made up their long friendship. For the rest of his life, they would swim to the surface of his consciousness. He would remember things about her he had forgotten. Each time would be agony.

"To your left," Qui-Gon said politely.

"Thank you," she murmured.

The woman reached for the door access panel and pushed the signal. The door slid open. She moved through and proceeded to the desk, which was straight ahead. Qui-Gon could now see that she was using a laser sensor device to guide her movements. As a Jedi, Tahl had decided to rely on her other senses so that she would not have to depend on such technology.

The woman spoke briefly to the clerk, who directed her in a loud, careful voice to a seat. Looking at the clerk's thin-faced, haughty expression, Qui-Gon sensed he would have trouble. He glanced at the clerk's name plate and walked forward.

"Good day, Vero," he said. "I'm hoping you can help me. My nephew Oleg is missing. I think he's a patient here. It would help if I knew —"

Vero interrupted him immediately. "No release of any med information without the proper authorization."

"I appreciate your attention to the rules," Qui-Gon said. "However —"

"No exceptions." Vero turned away. He barked out the name of the next patient, ignoring Qui-Gon.

This was certainly a different experience. In the other clinics, he'd found sympathetic clerks who had listened to his story and tried to help him. Qui-Gon could have used the Force on Vero, but he knew that everyone in the clinic was listening. If the rude Vero suddenly changed his approach, they would think it odd. Still, he wasn't about to walk away without finding out what he needed to know.

Suddenly a loud clatter came from behind him. The blind woman had upset her chair, then the one next to her. She began to try to right them, getting in the way of another patient. An argument began.

"Stop, stop! This is a clinic! What are you doing? Don't touch that! Don't move!" Vero hurried around the counter, upset at the commotion.

With a keen gaze, Qui-Gon saw the woman deliberately upset a flower vase.

"Not my ginkas!" Vero screamed, diving for the flowers.

She was doing it for him, Qui-Gon knew. She was giving him a little time.

He reached over the counter and swiveled Vero's datascreen to face him. Quickly, he clicked in Oleg's name. To his relief, his records showed up. Oleg had given an address close to the clinic. His next appointment was in two weeks.

Qui-Gon quickly swiveled the datascreen back into position. He walked past Vero, who was picking up flowers and scolding the woman for upsetting them. Qui-Gon righted a chair and gave a hand to the woman to help her sit down. He bent close to her ear. "Thanks for your help."

"You know when to give help, and when not to," she said. "That's rare."

"I had a good teacher."

Qui-Gon walked out quickly. The door slid shut behind him, sealing off the commotion. He had memorized the address and remembered the street, which he'd passed on the way to the clinic. Qui-Gon quickly made his way there.

The address was a small hotel. Qui-Gon asked for Oleg and was told he had checked out, but to try the café around the corner. A bit surprised that Oleg was not more discreet, Qui-Gon headed to the café.

The owner was wiping down tables in the front. Qui-Gon asked for Oleg and was directed to a table in the rear.

A slight, blond man sat at the table, his hands curled around a cup of juice. Qui-Gon sat down opposite him.

"It's about time," Oleg said nervously. "I've put myself in danger every minute."

"I got here as soon as I could," Qui-Gon said. Obviously, Oleg had been waiting for someone he did not know. That explained why he hadn't bothered to use an assumed name. It was just as apparent to Qui-Gon that this young man was not used to dealing with danger. His head constantly swiveled, looking for trouble. Anyone looking for him would have picked him out immediately.

"I have the file," Oleg said. "It's not on me, but it's not far. But I'm warning you, if you try anything, I'm prepared to shoot. I have to up the price."

"Why?" Qui-Gon asked. He would play this

out. He assumed, of course, that Oleg was talking about the list. He didn't want to buy it from him. If Oleg still had it, that meant that Balog didn't.

"I have to leave the planet," Oleg said, wiping his wet forehead with his napkin. "Do you think this is easy? Too many people are searching for me now."

"I might be able to come up with more," Qui-Gon said.

"Decide now," Oleg snapped. "I have no time to waste." His comlink signaled, and he listened for a moment. With his eyes on Qui-Gon, he replied, "Yes, that's right. I still have it. Will you meet my price? Good. I'll meet you there, then. Can't you make it earlier? All right."

He shut off the comlink. "There are others who will pay, as you see," he said. "I made an appointment, but you can buy it first. So decide. It's now or never."

"Never," Qui-Gon said. "The price is just too high. Sorry." He stood.

Oleg looked even more nervous. "Listen, I don't have to sell to this guy. I don't like him. He's an Absolute, and I hate them. They ruined my health. I'd rather the list end up with a Worker, believe me. I look like a traitor, but I'm just looking out for myself. Maybe we can negotiate."

"Sorry," Qui-Gon said again. He turned and left the café. He positioned himself out of sight of Oleg, but was able to see him through the reflection of the café window. Was the bidder on the comlink Balog? He had a strong feeling it was. Oleg had broken out into a sweat. And he had said he didn't want the list in the hands of the Absolutes.

Qui-Gon was close now. He could feel it. All his concentration was centered on that slight, nervous man in the café. The anger and grief he had compressed into a burning ball inside him threatened to flame up, and he tamped it down. Patience, he chided himself. Balog would be his very soon.

CHAPTER 6

Qui-Gon did not think it possible that a being could nurse a glass of juice as long as Oleg. He did not seem to notice the surly stare of the café owner, or the press of customers who came in, looking for a table as the café grew crowded.

Qui-Gon began to feel conspicuous, so he moved down the alley to another window. After a few minutes he moved to the back, where he could see the interior through a small, grimy window. He kept up his post there, pretending to loiter until people began to come home from work and windows lit up across the alley. Qui-Gon headed back to the front and crossed the street. He stationed himself at a juice bar with a good angle on the front of the café. Dusk fell. His patience wore thin. Was the conversation a bluff? Had Oleg merely been trying to get Qui-Gon to meet his price?

Qui-Gon was beginning to consider approaching Oleg again when he saw him head out of the café, glancing nervously over his shoulder. Qui-Gon joined the stream of people on the walkway and followed him.

At first, it was easy to keep Oleg in sight. The people on the streets were good cover. But as Oleg crossed over into the Worker Sector, the crowd grew larger. Oleg was a slight young man, and he soon got lost in the crowd. It was difficult to keep him in sight without running into him.

Gradually, Qui-Gon became aware that he was not the only one tailing Oleg. He did not turn his head or alter his stride in any way, but he threw his attention around him like a net. Someone was tailing Oleg from across the street.

It was Balog. He saw him reflected in the shiny surface of an approaching landspeeder. He recognized the stocky frame, the way the muscular legs seemed to power the body forward like a machine, not a man.

Qui-Gon did not know if Balog had seen him. Perhaps his focus was on Oleg. If he was lucky, that would be the case. But he could not rely on luck. His heart began to pound, and he had to discipline himself to keep his focus. He wanted to turn and rush at Balog in a full-scale attack. He wanted to make him pay for every breath

Tahl had struggled to take, every second her life systems slowly failed. He would make each moment of Balog's suffering an eternity. . . .

Where did that thought come from? The ferocity of it shocked him. It had risen from the depths of him. It sounded like vengeance. He did not know such an emotion could exist inside him. The knowledge made him uneasy.

I can control it. It will not take me over. I can capture Balog and not let my anger overtake me.

He said the words to himself, just the way he would have said them to Obi-Wan. He was a Jedi. His training would keep him on the right path. It had to.

His hands trembled, and he clasped them together for a moment. *Help me, Tahl,* he said fervently. He had never said such a thing to her when she was alive, though now he realized how many times he had gone to her for help. She had known that it was hard for him to ask for it. It was the one thing she had never teased him about. Instead, she had simply given him whatever he needed: information, assurance, compassion.

To his left, Balog speeded up. Qui-Gon melted back. Now he must keep both Balog and Oleg in sight.

Oleg entered a warehouse. Balog hurried

down an alley to the side of the building. There was no question in Qui-Gon's mind which one to pursue. He headed down the alley after Balog.

When he got to the back, he found himself in a small fenced area. It was empty. All the windows looking out from the warehouse were dark. Qui-Gon tried the door. It was locked.

It was a flicker in the corner of his eye that alerted him, nothing more. But it was enough. He was already turning and had his lightsaber activated when the first probe droid attacked. Blaster fire pinged by his ear. He felt the scorch near his shoulder. He reached up to bring it down with a swipe, but it veered off.

Blaster fire to his left, then to his right. Behind him. Qui-Gon counted seven droids, now in attack mode. Their sensors glowed red as they pinpointed his location. Blaster fire rained around him like a cage. It was almost impossible to dodge it.

Qui-Gon ran at the wire fence. He shifted his body horizontally, calling on the Force to help him scale it without using his hands. His balance was perfect as he hit the top. He gave a backward leap and took two probe droids out with one single downward stroke.

Before he hit the ground, he twisted in midair

to land a few centimeters away, confusing the probe droid that fired at the spot where he should have landed. He ran at the warehouse wall now, straight up, and then flipped backward, swiping a glancing blow at the third droid. It buzzed, blaster fire erupting in a series of flashes. Then it began to smoke, spiraling down until it crashed.

Qui-Gon fought in a frenzy, mindful that Balog was inside that warehouse. The probe droids were slowing him down, and frustration boiled inside him at their insistent buzzing.

He attacked with a new ferocity. He launched himself off the fence, kicking out with one leg to send one droid flying while thrusting a blow straight into the heart of another. It gave an anguished squawk and fell to the ground at top speed, crashing and bursting into flames.

Qui-Gon hit the ground, lightsaber held high, ready for the next challenge. But to his surprise, the remaining two probe droids suddenly wheeled away and flew off into the darkness.

He didn't hesitate a moment. He cut a hole in the locked door with his lightsaber and charged through. He ran down the corridor, searching room after room. The rooms were filled with tools, equipment, and durasteel bins. He found nothing until he ran into a small room near the turbolift.

There was Oleg, lying on the floor, arms outstretched, mouth open. He had a surprised expression on his face. But he would never feel surprised again.

CHAPTER 7

Mace had not shown any emotion when Obi-Wan gave him the news of Qui-Gon's disappearance. He had simply nodded. "We will hear from him, I'm sure," he had said.

But when they discovered that Qui-Gon had switched off his comlink, Mace's disapproval was obvious.

"We must proceed without Qui-Gon," he said. "I think we should split up. I'll go to the United Legislature and gather information. Obi-Wan, can you find this medic, Yanci? We need another copy of that list."

"I think so," Obi-Wan said. "She said she was staying with the Workers, and I can trace her through Irini and Lenz."

"Good. Then you and Bant must find her and join Qui-Gon in tracking Oleg. No doubt you could run into Qui-Gon at the same time. As soon as you find either Oleg or Qui-Gon, contact me."

Obi-Wan nodded. Mace left them, hurrying out of Manex's residence and striding down the street. Some of the passersby glared at him, seeing his Jedi robes. No doubt they had heard the rumors being spread of Jedi treachery. Obi-Wan was certain Mace noticed this, but he walked on with no hesitation visible in his stride or expression.

"Where are we headed?" Bant asked. There was a new crispness in her voice.

"The Worker Sector," Obi-Wan said. "We can catch a public transport this way."

As they walked, Obi-Wan thought he could not bear it if they weren't able to be friends again. He needed things to be open and easy with Bant. With Qui-Gon gone, things were so confused. He was worried about the reason Qui-Gon left without him. Was Qui-Gon driven by vengeance? Was that why he hadn't wanted Obi-Wan along?

Obi-Wan missed his Master. It was hard to have to miss his friend, too. Especially when she walked beside him.

They swung aboard an almost empty airbus. Obi-Wan looked out at the streets as they passed, hoping to catch a glimpse of his Master.

"He's out there somewhere," he said. He

didn't know if Bant was speaking to him, but he was so in the habit of confiding in her that the words tumbled out before he could stop them. "And I don't know what he's thinking or planning. He could be walking into danger. He could need me. If anything happens . . ."

Bant turned cool silver eyes on him. "If anything happens to your Master, you'll feel as I do." She turned her face forward again.

Obi-Wan felt as though she had slapped him. Of course she was right.

What was there to say? He had already apologized. He felt sincerely sorry he had not considered Bant's feelings. The only thing he could do was agree.

"Yes," he said. "Then I'd know exactly how you feel."

It was rare on a mission when something went exactly the way it should. Yet this time, luck was with them. Obi-Wan remembered exactly where he and Qui-Gon had gone to meet Lenz. It had only been a few days before, but it felt like a lifetime ago. Luckily Lenz was still living in the same quarters. He usually moved often to escape the surveillance of the new Absolutes.

Lenz willingly gave them the address where Yanci was staying a short distance away. Yanci greeted Obi-Wan with tired affection and printed out a copy of the list on a durasheet. They were back on the street and heading for the address of the first med clinic in a short period of time.

They had no trouble with the first three clinics. The clerks freely told them that Oleg was not a patient. But the fourth clinic was staffed by an arrogant clerk named Vero. Puffed up with self-importance, he refused to give out any information.

"I don't know what med clinics do in the Worker Sector," he said haughtily, "but here, we are Civilized, and take our jobs seriously." He eyed Bant with disdain. "Obviously, you are new here. On your planet, things are no doubt more primitive. You might not be familiar with our procedures."

Bant's skin flushed pink with anger. "Listen, you —"

"Thank you," Obi-Wan said quickly, pulling Bant away from the desk.

"Getting into a confrontation isn't going to help," he whispered to her. "We'll have to think of another way."

Bant eyed the clerk. "How about lightsabers? Is that *primitive* enough for him?"

Obi-Wan grinned. Bant was the most gentle creature he knew, but she had her limits. "He's probably never seen a Mon Calamari before," he said. "New Apsolon doesn't get many tourists. There are plenty of good Civilized, but I'm sure there are plenty of ones like Vero, too."

"How are you at using the Force to affect his mind?" Bant asked, frowning. "I don't know if I could manage it. Vero is stupid, but he seems stubborn."

Obi-Wan doubted that he would be successful, either. "And the waiting room is so small — everyone would overhear," he murmured.

Bant's silver gaze roved over the group. "Everyone is staring at us."

"They've probably never seen a Mon Calamari before, either," Obi-Wan pointed out.

Something sparked in Bant's eyes. "That gives me an idea."

Suddenly, she weaved and began to gasp. "I'm over my limit," she said. "Help me. I need water."

Obi-Wan supported her as she slumped over. "Water!" she cried.

Vero looked over at them, his expression a mix of irritation and alarm. "What is it? The medics are busy."

"She's a Mon Calamari," Obi-Wan said frantically. "She can't stay out of water for more than four hours. We need to immerse her, now!"

"I can't authorize that," Vero said, shaking his head. "She'll just have to wait."

"She'll die!" Obi-Wan cried. Bant cooperated by slumping down even farther.

"I've heard about Mon Calamari," someone spoke up from the waiting area. "What he says is true."

"This will be on your record!" Obi-Wan warned Vero. He'd nearly said *conscience,* but he wasn't sure if Vero had one. "Do you want that?"

At the mention of his record, Vero looked alarmed. "All right, all right," he said. "There's an immersion tub in back. I'll take her."

Obi-Wan handed Bant over to Vero, who took her arm with distaste. He half dragged her back toward the med cubicles.

Obi-Wan wasted no time. He moved stealthfully to the desk and quickly accessed the holofiles.

Yes! Oleg had been here, just a few days before. And there was an address listed. Obi-Wan quickly memorized it, then hurried back. He slid into a seat in the waiting area just as Vero returned.

"Your friend is having her swim," Vero said with a frown.

Bant emerged a few minutes later, still damp. Obi-Wan nodded at her to let her know he had succeeded. Quickly, they left the clinic and headed for a street map kiosk on a nearby corner. They pinpointed the address. It was only a few blocks away. The address was for a small hotel, but their search ended when they discovered that Oleg had checked out.

"Too many questions about that one," the owner of the hotel said darkly. "And I've got no answers for you."

Disappointed, Obi-Wan stopped on the walkway outside. He had a feeling that Qui-Gon had not given up so easily.

"I guess we could stake the place out," Bant said dubiously. "Or stake out the clinic."

"His next appointment isn't for two weeks," Obi-Wan said, discouraged.

"Well, let's contact Mace and tell him it's a dead end," Bant suggested.

Obi-Wan wasn't thrilled at giving Mace that news, but he reached for his comlink.

When Mace answered, he quickly explained the steps they had taken and where they were.

Mace sounded odd. "Give me your location again." When Obi-Wan repeated it, there was a long pause. "I've just received word that a body was found nearby. Meet me there. I am leaving now." Mace gave Obi-Wan the address and signed off.

Obi-Wan looked over at Bant. He knew what

they both feared. He could not speak the fear aloud, but it rose inside him, draining him of strength. The body was Qui-Gon.

Without a word, they turned and ran toward the address Mace had given them. It was only a few blocks away.

They stopped in front of a warehouse. Security vehicles were parked outside, and officers walked in and out.

Obi-Wan strode forward as if he belonged there. He couldn't wait another second.

"We are Jedi. Manex has given us the authority to investigate," he said firmly.

To his surprise, the security officer waved them inside. Manex must have followed through and demanded access for the Jedi.

The body lay under a tarp in the hallway. Obi-Wan felt relief drain the remaining strength from his muscles. He could already tell from the outlines that the body was too short and slight to be Qui-Gon's.

He bent over and lifted a corner of the tarp anyway. Mild blue eyes stared up at him in surprise. No matter how many times Obi-Wan had seen it, he never got used to death.

He guessed who the young man was. "Do you have an ID?" he asked a nearby officer.

"Name was Oleg," the officer replied as he entered something into a datapad.

"Was anything on the body?" Bant asked.

"Just a blaster. Never got a chance to use it, did he? A probe droid got him first."

While they waited for Mace, Obi-Wan and Bant explored the area. At first they found nothing to indicate a struggle, no clues to send them in a new direction. Then they came to the back door. The panel was peeled back, leaving an opening wide enough for a man to step through.

Mace's voice came from behind them. "A light-saber, no doubt."

"It could have been a vibrotorch," Obi-Wan suggested. Suddenly he did not want Mace to think that Qui-Gon had been there.

Mace didn't answer. His eyes narrowed, and he moved forward to pluck something off the sharp end of a broken hinge. He held it up to Obi-Wan and Bant. It was a piece of a Jedi robe.

He turned and looked through the opening cut in the door. The security officers had left bright glow rods to illuminate the back area.

"There was a battle with probe droids," Mace said. "See the scorch marks on the pavement? Maybe four or five — or even more." He turned to Obi-Wan. "Did Qui-Gon employ probe droids to track Balog?"

Obi-Wan swallowed. He could not lie to Mace. "Yes," he said.

Mace stood holding the scrap of fabric. His face showed nothing of what he was thinking. But Obi-Wan could guess.

Was Qui-Gon involved in Oleg's death? Had his grief and rage turned him to the dark side? Would he not care who was in his way in his quest to avenge Tahl's death? Obi-Wan feared the question was in Mace's mind. His bigger worry was that it was in his own.

CHAPTER 8

Qui-Gon moved swiftly through the dark streets. The clue he had found at the site of Oleg's killing led him on. By Oleg's side, he had found a slender chain and pendant. The chain had been broken. He had recognized the pendant immediately. Irini had been at the warehouse.

He stood for a moment outside Lenz's dwelling, wondering how to proceed. Irini did not volunteer information freely. But his impatience allowed no time for persuasion.

Then he saw Irini heading toward him, her arms filled with a bag of food. Her steps slowed for an instant when she saw Qui-Gon. Then she moved forward briskly to hide her hesitation. In that moment, Qui-Gon decided that his best chance was to bluff.

"So we meet again tonight," he said.

She eyed him warily. "Again?"

"You were at the warehouse tonight with Oleg. So was I."

She swallowed. Her eyes narrowed. "What do you want?"

"Did you get the list?"

She let out a breath. "No. He didn't have it. I posed as a buyer, hoping to get it. If not, I wanted to protect him."

"But he betrayed the Workers," Qui-Gon said.

"He saw a way to make his fortune, yes," Irini said wearily. "Many Workers are desperate that way. Despite our hopes, the wealth of the Civilized has not trickled down to us. But Oleg is still a Worker, and we know he was being pursued. My job was to bring him in."

"Did you see what happened?" Qui-Gon asked.

"Two probe droids attacked, so I got out," she said. "I'm sure it was Balog who sent them."

"Balog was there, too," Qui-Gon said. "I saw him."

Irini dropped the bundle she held. Fruit and protein packs spilled onto the pavement. "Balog was there? Did he get the list?"

"You said Oleg didn't have it," Qui-Gon said.

She shook her head rapidly, suddenly concerned. "I didn't see it. But maybe I overlooked something . . ."

"I don't think Oleg had the list on him," Qui-

Gon said. "He was worried about his safety. I also think it's possible that he'd already sold it."

"Then why would he meet another buyer?" Irini asked.

"As you say, he wanted his fortune," Qui-Gon said. "He could sell the list several times and make enough to live out the rest of his life in luxury."

Irini pressed a hand against her eyes. "So several people could have the list, then. I hadn't thought of that."

"The question is: *who?*" Qui-Gon said. "And if Balog does have it, what is his next move?"

"I can't answer those questions. I'm as much in the dark as you are." Irini bent down and began to retrieve her food. Qui-Gon bent to help her.

"We are after the same thing, Irini," he said, placing a package of tea into her bag. "It might be a good idea if you helped me."

Suddenly a look of sadness came over Irini's usually impassive face. "I would if I could," she said. "I have to get these to Lenz now." Then, cradling the package in her arms, she walked off.

Qui-Gon contemplated his next move. It was hard to keep his mind clear. He felt as though he were stumbling around in the dark. So much of his pursuit of Balog was based on guesswork.

But it was all he had.

The list was still the key. Even if Balog had it, his next move would be to consolidate his power. If Oleg had already sold it, who would be in the market to buy it?

The answer was easy. New elections were about to be held. Those who would benefit most by the list, or be the most threatened by it, would be politicians. A Legislator who held that list would hold great power.

He hated to admit it, but Mace had been right. He needed to go to the United Legislature. It was night now; he wouldn't have much luck finding Legislators. But surely there was something he could accomplish. Qui-Gon turned and headed back to the Civilized Sector.

CHAPTER 9

Obi-Wan and Bant stood outside the Luster, an opulent café near the United Legislature building. Inside under the great domed lamps they could see the elite Civilized at polished tables, laughing, eating, and talking, their heads together in government gossip. Chairs were drawn up at already crowded tables, making it difficult to move around the room, but no one seemed to mind.

Mace was somewhere inside, trying to gather information. He had said that the two could wait in more comfortable quarters at Manex's residence, but neither Obi-Wan nor Bant wanted to leave. There was a feeling of urgency, as though every moment counted.

Bant stood, her arms folded, her eyes on the brilliantly lit café. Obi-Wan wondered how to start a conversation. Suddenly, after years of talking to Bant about everything that was on his mind, he had to struggle to find something to say.

Bant held her slight body rigid. Her stare was as fierce as Mace's. Her stiffness and concentration made it even harder for him to break the silence.

Then he noticed that she was not as contained as she appeared. Her hands were gripped together tightly. He realized that far from being lost in concentration, Bant was struggling to maintain her composure.

When he looked closer, he saw that her eyes were full of tears. She was struggling to keep them from falling.

"Bant." He said her name gently. He didn't know what else to say.

"She should be here," Bant said in a choked voice. "It seems impossible that she's not here. I can't believe she won't come around the corner any second. I keep hearing her scold us for making such a big fuss and coming here to save her." The tears tumbled down her face. "It hurts so much, Obi-Wan. I can't find peace in her death. I know I'm supposed to accept it. I can't."

It was the longest flood of words she had spoken since she'd arrived. Obi-Wan realized that Bant had said all the things he had been feeling. It *did* seem impossible that Tahl was dead. He knew that part of him hadn't absorbed it.

He knew that he was focusing on his worries about Qui-Gon so that he wouldn't have to.

"I know what you mean," he said. "When we found her, and she was so weak, I never for one moment thought she could die. Tahl was so strong. She was as strong as Qui-Gon."

"Did she say anything?" Bant asked timidly. "Anything before . . ."

"She was too weak to talk when I saw her," Obi-Wan said. "Qui-Gon was with her when she died."

"I'm glad such a good friend was there," Bant said.

Obi-Wan hesitated. He did not know whether he should speak. But didn't he owe Bant his confidence? Maybe it would help to close the gap between them.

"I think Qui-Gon and Tahl had become more than friends," he told her. "Here on New Apsolon, something changed. That's why Qui-Gon is grieving the way he is."

Bant turned, surprised. "You mean they loved each other?"

Obi-Wan nodded.

Bant looked down at her clasped hands. "Then it is even more sad, isn't it?"

"Yes," Obi-Wan said. "It's the saddest thing I've ever seen. That's why I'm worried about Qui-Gon."

Bant reached out and squeezed his arm. Obi-Wan was happy to feel the spontaneous gesture. "We will help him, Obi-Wan," she promised. And for the first time, Obi-Wan felt that maybe they could.

Just then Mace emerged from the café, his robe swirling around his ankles. He crossed the road and came up to them.

"I haven't learned much," he admitted. "But I did pick up an item of interesting gossip as I was leaving. Just today Legislator Pleni has announced that she will run for Supreme Governor. She has kept a low profile in the Legislature, so this was surprising. In just an afternoon, she managed to sway some powerful Legislators to support her."

Mace saw the look of puzzlement on the faces of Bant and Obi-Wan. "Her sudden bid for power and the quick support she received could mean that she bought the list from Oleg," he told them. "At any rate, it is worth investigating." Mace gathered his cloak around him. "If she has the list, she could be in danger. Whoever has possession of it could end up like Oleg. Come. Her residence is not far."

Mace's long stride covered more distance than Obi-Wan could make at a slow run. He and Bant had to jog to keep up with him.

Legislator Pleni lived alone in a small, elegant dwelling made of the gray stone that so much of New Apsolon was built with. All the lights inside the house were on. Mace pressed the illuminated bar that would alert her that she had visitors. They waited by the panel to announce themselves, but there was no answer.

"She could have left the lights on when she went out," Mace said. "But let's explore just the same."

The look on his face was uneasy. Mace had a deep connection to the Force. Obi-Wan had felt nothing, but now he focused his attention on the Force, reaching out around him. He did not pick up anything.

They walked around the perimeter of the dwelling. Mace seemed to grow more worried as they walked. When they reached the back, Obi-Wan felt it, too — a disturbance in the Force. He glanced at Mace, who saw traces of a probe droid's entry into a high window.

The door was secured, but Mace didn't hesitate. He cut a hole in it with his lightsaber and strode in. Obi-Wan and Bant followed.

The stone floors gleamed. Not an item seemed out of place. They walked through the empty rooms in the eerie silence. Then they mounted the stairs.

Upstairs, they finally saw evidence of a struggle. Furniture was overturned. Large crystal vases were smashed.

Mace looked up to the ceiling. He pointed to several smudge marks. "Probe droids."

The disturbance in the Force was now more than a ripple for Obi-Wan. It was a cresting wave. He moved forward, his hand on his lightsaber hilt. He turned a corner into Legislator Pleni's bedroom. It was untouched except for a halfway ajar door riddled with blaster fire.

Obi-Wan walked forward slowly, dreading what he would find behind that door. He nudged it open with the toe of his boot.

Legislator Pleni lay curled up in the corner, her hands clutching a blaster. A probe droid lay at her feet. She was dead.

Mace came up behind him noiselessly. Obi-Wan heard his deep sigh.

"We are always one step too late on New Apsolon," Mace said. Obi-Wan could locate in his voice the determination that this would no longer be the case.

They heard noises below, and the sound of feet on the stairs. Minutes later, a security squad burst in.

"She is in here," Mace said.

He brought Obi-Wan and Bant downstairs, where the evidence of Legislator Pleni's horrible death was not in front of their eyes. They were questioned by the security squad, then told they were free to go. Still, Mace lingered.

When the security squad came downstairs at last, having completed its investigation, Mace stopped the head officer.

"Any conclusions?"

"Yes," the officer said, brushing past them.

Mace stood in front of him, effectively blocking his path. "You know that Manex has ordered the security squads to cooperate with the Jedi."

The officer hesitated. A gleam of malice lit up his eyes. "Fine. Let me tell you what we discovered then. Legislator Pleni was killed by a probe droid. We have been able to trace its owner."

"You have a name?" Mace Windu asked.

"Certainly." The security officer bared his teeth in a smile. "Your Jedi friend, Qui-Gon Jinn."

CHAPTER 10

Qui-Gon got started early the next morning. He had spent most of the night going from café to café, trying to gather information. As the hours got later, tongues grew looser, but he did not discover anything that put him on Balog's track. Gossip swirled about Alani's bid for the Supreme Governor position and a growing swell of support for Manex. Neither helped him at all.

He spent the rest of the night on a bench in a grassy park, impatiently waiting for dawn. He could feel Balog out there, maneuvering, scheming, plotting his next move. He could feel the absence of Tahl as an ache so deep he could not face it directly. When he thought of her last days, what Balog had put her through, he would have to move, have to get up and walk through the park, driving himself to exhaustion so that he would not think of the dark vengeance that burned inside him. He would have to conquer it . . . somehow. He pushed his mind to numbness. It was the only way he could go on. Before long he had explored every path in the large urban park. He could draw a map of it blindfolded.

The suns rose, and people began to trickle out into the streets. Qui-Gon saw the morning begin with relief. He went to a café across from the Legislature for a light breakfast and watched and waited until the official buildings were full of people beginning their day.

Qui-Gon was still dressed in a traveler's cape over his tunic. He hoped he would not be recognizable as a Jedi. He decided to pose as a businessman looking for new opportunities on New Apsolon.

Just as he was about to leave, he overheard a conversation behind him. Two aides had just greeted each other. He heard the name "Legislator Pleni." And then he heard the name "Qui-Gon Jinn."

Qui-Gon bent over, pretending to sip his tea, while he filtered out the noise of the café and concentrated on the conversation behind him. He then received the unwelcome shock of discovering that he was wanted for the murder of a Legislator.

Which might make his intelligence-gathering plans in official buildings of the Legislature this morning more difficult than he had anticipated. Qui-Gon had great respect for the security officers on New Apsolon. He was certain that every one of them had a detailed physical description of him. And the Legislature's offices were guarded by security officers.

Qui-Gon's hands curled around his teacup. He had to place them in his lap. The urge to smash the cup into tiny pieces was too great. It seemed that every time he wanted to take a step forward, he was kicked a step back.

He let out air through his nose, breathing quietly and steadily. He was not thinking like a Jedi. Frustration must be controlled. There was always a way.

The streets were still crowded, but he needed to keep moving. He also needed a better disguise than a cloak. He could not hide his size, but he could transform himself in different ways. Qui-Gon left the café and went shopping.

Within a half hour, he had transformed himself into a dark-eyed businessman in a veda cloth robe. His long hair was concealed by a wrapped cloth headpiece favored by the elite of the planet of Rorgam. He had found it in a small shop selling used items. It would be good cover to pose as a citizen of Rorgam, a world made up of immigrants from many different worlds.

Qui-Gon headed for the halls of the Legislature. Because New Apsolon was a tech center for this corner of the galaxy, many deals were made here. With the growing instability of the planet, there was a certain frenzy in the air.

A security officer stood at the first checkpoint. Qui-Gon had no choice but to walk through. If he couldn't walk through the hallways without a challenge, he wouldn't be able to do anything.

He was relieved when he made it past the security officer, who merely gave him a bland look and moved his gaze to sweep the visitor behind him. He was lucky that Manex had not instituted higher security procedures that required text docs for admittance.

There were several things he needed to know. Why was he a suspect in Pleni's death? He had never heard of her until that morning. Was her death connected to Oleg's? Had she, too, tried to buy the list? Qui-Gon decided that the only course open to him was to present himself as a possible buyer as well. If the word got out that a prosperous businessman from Rorgam had money to spend, sooner or later someone would come forward with something to sell.

Drawing his robe around him, Qui-Gon plunged into the throng.

He was deep in conversation with an important Legislative aide when he saw Eritha and

Alani heading down the hall. Alani was talking with a group of admirers who clustered closely around her. To his relief, they turned off down the hall. Eritha brought up the rear, and she spotted Qui-Gon. A look of surprise, then greeting, came over her face. Qui-Gon ignored her.

Eritha hesitated. Then her face smoothed out and became emotionless when she realized he did not want her to recognize him. All of this took only a beat of a moment. Once again Qui-Gon had cause to admire Eritha's cleverness. The girl had good reflexes.

Eritha signaled him discreetly and moved into a side hall. Qui-Gon wrapped up his conversation with the aide and casually strolled after her.

The hallway was empty, and she made sure he had followed before accessing a door. He followed her inside into a small conference room.

To his surprise, Eritha threw herself in his arms. "I'm so glad to see you," she said. "I was so worried." He patted her shoulder, and she stepped back. "You shouldn't be here. Do you know that you're wanted for murder?"

Qui-Gon nodded. "Do you know why? I've never met Legislator Pleni. Did Balog set this up?"

"I don't know," Eritha said. "Possibly. I know

that Alani is still in touch with him. I'm here try-ing to get information. I think I have a lead. But I have to be careful. I don't want Alani to sus-pect, so I'm pretending to completely support her candidacy. And there's a rumor going around the Legislature that you should know about. Manex has the list of secret Absolute informers."

"Manex?"

Eritha nodded. "I have a feeling that Roan's brother is more ambitious than he pretends. He wants to hold on to his power."

"I'll need to be able to get in touch with you," Qui-Gon told her. "I'll be moving around fre-quently."

Eritha bit her lip. "Can you wait here for just a few minutes? I'm close to finding out where Balog is hiding. This conference room isn't used much anymore. I can be back within ten minutes."

"If you're delayed —"

"I won't be," Eritha said confidently, and hur-ried out the door.

Qui-Gon sighed. Eritha had all the impatience and optimism of youth. If she didn't return, he would have no way to get in touch with her. He would have to sneak into the Supreme Governor's residence.

There was nothing to do but wait. He could

spare ten or fifteen minutes. Qui-Gon settled himself into a chair, going over what had happened that morning. He had dropped hints about how he was looking to buy power and would pay handsomely for it. He had even hinted at the existence of a list. Now and then he had caught a spark of interest in a Legislator or an aide, but he wasn't sure if it was based on knowledge or simply on pure greed.

Five minutes passed. Qui-Gon got up restlessly and went to the window. He looked down below at the crowded street beyond the Legislature wall. Was Balog moving about freely, or was he hiding during the daylight hours, letting his allies like Alani prepare the way for his return?

The door hissed open. But instead of Eritha, a confused-looking aide stood in the doorway. "I'm sorry — isn't this where the Rock Mining Development Act subcommittee is meeting?"

"I'm afraid not," Qui-Gon said.

"Oh. Sorry again." The young man nodded and withdrew, and the door hissed shut behind him.

An innocent interruption, Qui-Gon thought. But perhaps not. He thought carefully about the young man's appearance. He wore the navy tunic of an aide, but . . .

His boots. They were the boots that the security officers wore. He was doing a check of the rooms. And he could have recognized Qui-Gon.

Qui-Gon withdrew his lightsaber in one quick motion. He would have to contact Eritha later. He cut a neat hole in the glass and stepped through onto the ledge. Using his cable launcher, he lowered himself down to the pavement behind the wall.

"There he is!" Chips from the wall flew as blaster fire hit on either side of him. Qui-Gon looked up. Two security officers aimed their blasters at him.

"Don't move!" one of them shouted.

Qui-Gon ran. He deflected the blaster fire as he zigzagged down the short passageway between the wall and the Legislative building. Then he leaped to the top of the wall and jumped over.

Pedestrians scattered as he landed. They looked at him curiously, but he matched his stride to theirs and continued walking. He increased his pace as they lost interest and turned down a side street. He weaved through the blocks surrounding the Legislature, finding a deserted alley to shed his overcloak and cap. No doubt a complete description of him was now updated on every security officer's datapad. He would blend in better in his traveler's cloak.

Qui-Gon caught a repulsorlift airbus and stayed on it until the end of the line. He resolved to go back and find Eritha under cover of darkness.

Balog had always been one step ahead of him. This time, he resolved that he would be first.

CHAPTER 11

The holotape of Tahl as an Absolute had hurt the Jedi. Qui-Gon's arrest warrant made it worse. Mace ran into roadblocks whenever he tried to gather information. The support of Manex was no longer enough.

Obi-Wan saw the frustration tighten Mace's features. He knew that Mace was deeply concerned that Qui-Gon had not surfaced to clear his name. He, too, wondered what his Master was thinking. In rare moments of rest, he reached out with the Force, trying desperately to connect. At times he thought he could feel Qui-Gon, but it was not a strong, clear sensation. It was murky and gray. He knew his effort to reach his Master through the Force would not work. They would not connect. There was too much unresolved emotion swirling around Qui-Gon, too much he was trying to hide.

"You need rest," Mace said at the end of a long, fruitless day. "Both of you."

But neither Bant nor Obi-Wan wanted to retire to their quarters. They sat in Manex's private sitting room. Since Manex's favorite color was green and he believed in indulging himself, every cushion, every seating area, was a different shade of the color. The floors were of highly polished black stone. Obi-Wan felt almost dizzy sitting in the center of all that bright color, but Manex had insisted on giving the Jedi his favorite room, and they felt they could not refuse.

Manex returned from the Legislature only a few moments after the Jedi had. He rushed into the room, his curls waving, looking agitated.

"Qui-Gon was spotted at the Legislature. There was a blaster battle."

Obi-Wan felt a silent cry of protest rise inside him. He couldn't bear it if something happened to Qui-Gon now. His body went instantly cold. Bant moved closer to him, her shoulder touching his.

Mace stood. "What happened?"

"He escaped, of course."

Obi-Wan let out a long breath. Qui-Gon was safe. He felt Bant relax a fraction, and she gave Obi-Wan a look of pure relief.

Manex mopped his brow with a pale gold

handkerchief. "What a day. I must tell you that there is a movement afoot to draft me for the elections. It is not a job that I seek. But I am thinking about it. Maybe it is time I got involved. I used to think my brother was the hero, the public servant. I used to say I was only here to make money." Manex shoved the handkerchief in his pocket. "Maybe I became the way I am because my brother was so noble. Now I am no longer sure what my role is. Maybe the time to abandon my principle of self-protection is here."

"What about Alani?" Obi-Wan asked. "Would it be hard for you to oppose her?" Manex did not know of Alani's tie to the Absolutes. He professed affection for the twins.

Manex hesitated. "I have to think of what is best for New Apsolon," he said. "And I've realized one thing. We cannot form a solid government — whether with me or another leader — if we do not expose Balog and the Absolutes. I have a plan."

Obi-Wan tried not to look dubious. He couldn't imagine what sort of plan Manex would devise.

"I will act as a decoy," he declared. "I'll let it be known that the list of secret informers has come into my possession."

Mace shook his head. "No, it's too dangerous. You realize what happened to the last two beings who claimed this?"

"They are dead. Yes, I realize this very well." Manex clasped his hands together. "I'm trying not to think about it. And, actually, you can't say no, because I've already spread the rumor."

Obi-Wan saw how Bant watched the faces of the two men. She usually did not speak in meetings, but she was the most intent listener he'd ever seen. He could learn from her stillness, he suddenly thought.

"This may not be wise," Mace said, frowning.

"You're telling me," Manex snorted. "I'm hardly a courageous man. But I'm hoping that with Jedi protection, I'll be all right. If we can get Balog to expose himself, we can catch him. Don't you want to clear Qui-Gon's name?"

"Of course. But it is not clear if this is the way to do it," Mace said.

"It is the only way," Manex insisted. "You know it is."

Obi-Wan's gaze went from Manex to Mace. Of course he knew that Mace had to agree to protect Manex. It had been a foolish move on Manex's part, but no one wanted Obi-Wan's opinion. Now they would have to baby-sit Manex in the hope that Balog would show up. Was that what Manex wanted? Did he want to tie up the Jedi's time until he could consolidate power? Perhaps he was in league with Balog.

Obi-Wan reminded himself that Qui-Gon had trusted Manex. He had gently pointed out that just because a man enjoyed his wealth did not make him a man of bad character. Qui-Gon had seen something likeable in Manex's happy pursuit of his own pleasures.

"All right, we'll protect you," Mace said. "But *we* will form the plan."

The lights were still powered down in the house, as a house of mourning. Manex sat at a table in his garden, nervously fiddling with a cup of "the finest juice on New Apsolon — can I fetch the Jedi some glasses?" The Jedi had long ago refused, and Manex had hardly been able to eat or drink himself.

"Look relaxed," Mace told him in a low tone.

"I'm trying," Manex said between his teeth.

Mace stood behind a screen of bushes. Obi-Wan was a few yards away. Bant was on the opposite side of the small clearing where Manex had laid stone over the grass for an outdoor seating area.

If there was to be an ambush, Mace wanted plenty of room to maneuver. He had decided that Manex would eat his evening meal outside and then linger as the suns set. Manex had picked at his food and now was making a weak attempt to sip his juice in a serene fashion. He only succeeded in spilling it down his tunic.

The suns set, and the darkness grew. Only a small light on the table illuminated the area. Obi-Wan kept himself attuned for the sound of probe droids approaching. He was determined not to let Balog slip through their fingers. Once he was in their hands, they would have justice for Tahl. And Qui-Gon would return. Obi-Wan would never admit it to anyone, but he would feel better if they were the ones to catch Balog, not Qui-Gon.

Mace had linked the house's security system to his comlink. It must have vibrated an alert, for he turned to Obi-Wan. "Security has been breached on the east wall," he said.

"What?" Manex asked.

"Move closer to us as though you are looking at the stars," Mace ordered quietly.

Manex pushed his chair back. He rose, still clutching his cup, and pretended to look at the sky. Obi-Wan knew that Mace wanted Manex close to cover if anything happened. There was a low stone wall that they could push him behind in just a few seconds.

Obi-Wan felt a surge in the Force and saw a shadow flit across the lawn. It could have been a night bird or a shadow across the moon. But it wasn't.

He and Mace sprang forward together. Bant came around the other side in a flanking motion. Obi-Wan pushed Manex behind the wall as he darted closer. Three lightsabers were activated as the Jedi advanced.

"Good to see you, too," Qui-Gon said, stepping into the light.

"Master!" Obi-Wan exclaimed.

He looked at Manex peeking over the wall at the three Jedi. "So I see it's a trap. Looks like I fell for it, not Balog."

"Qui-Gon," Mace began sternly, "what are you —"

He stopped abruptly. He and Qui-Gon looked toward the front of the dwelling. It took another beat or two, but Obi-Wan heard it, too. Angry pounding at the front door. A few seconds later Obi-Wan saw security forces pounding down the hall while Manex's protocol droid waved his arms in protest.

Mace hurried forward, saying over his shoulder to Qui-Gon, "I suggest you find another exit."

Drawing his robes around him, Mace quickly entered the house. They heard the angry voice of a security officer.

"I know he is here. We have our proof! He

bought the probe droid that killed Legislator Pleni!"

Qui-Gon was screened by the elaborate bushes of the grounds. He hesitated, listening to the officer.

"Qui-Gon, you must go," Obi-Wan urged. "I'll come with you."

Qui-Gon hesitated. He met Obi-Wan's gaze. "No. I'm sorry I've caused you worry, Padawan," he said. "I must do this my way."

"But —" Obi-Wan began. Before he could finish, he felt his words snatched away by the wind, even before he had a chance to form them.

Qui-Gon had become a shadow again, moving across the soft green grass. Then he disappeared.

CHAPTER 12

Qui-Gon ran through the darkness, grateful for the new moons that made the night so dark. He moved from shadow to shadow noiselessly. When he had put a good deal of distance between himself and Manex's residence, he finally slowed down.

He was tired, but he wanted to run again. Pushing his body was the only time his mind had a chance to empty out. Facing Mace had been difficult. Facing Obi-Wan had been worse. He knew he belonged with the Jedi. Yet he could not seem to stop himself from going on alone. His emotions were too large right now, too raw. Around the Jedi he felt too exposed. Mace would see how difficult it was for him to maintain serenity. He could even order Qui-Gon back to the Temple. Qui-Gon could not allow that.

The truth was, he dreaded the moment he

would walk back into the Temple and know that Tahl's footsteps would never echo in its halls again. The Temple would never again welcome him in the same way. Loss would be as much a part of it as shelter.

His fever to catch Balog battled with his fear of the future, when this mission would be over. He would be faced with only his grief to bear, and he would have to look ahead to empty years. What would happen to him then?

A deep chill caused him to shudder. The cool wind was drying his sweat. He saw a security patrol ahead and quickly turned down a side street. Once again he would not sleep tonight. He would have to keep alert. Every officer in the city was now looking for Qui-Gon Jinn.

But he had learned something. They had tied him to the murder through the probe droids. He could not understand why the probe droids had attacked someone instead of tracking Balog, as they had been programmed to do. He wondered if the two droids that had veered off when attacking him had actually been his own droids. It had been strange that they had suddenly gone away. Did that mean that his droids had attacked Oleg, too? Someone had reprogrammed them.

He needed answers, and for once he knew where to find them. He would pay a visit to the black-market dealer, Mota, who had sold him the droids. If they were reprogrammed, Mota was undoubtedly the link to whoever reprogrammed them. And if that person was Balog, he might have a way to contact him.

Qui-Gon circled back and glanced down the street. The security officer was gone. He struck out across the road into the park. There were more places to hide here in case he was spotted. And cutting across the park would bring him closer to the Worker Sector.

Qui-Gon suddenly sensed that someone was behind him, matching his footsteps and trying to match his speed. Qui-Gon melted off into the trees. He made an arc and came up behind his pursuer. He saw a glint of gold hair in the darkness. It was Eritha.

He strode forward and grasped her arm. She gasped, then saw it was him. She was breathing hard, as if she'd just had a hard run. "I've been following you since you left Manex," she said. "Or at least I've been trying to. I lost you and kept circling around. Finally I thought I saw you enter the park."

"Why are you following me?"

She leaned over, trying to catch her breath. Her braids were unraveling, and her face was flushed.

"Does Manex have the list?"

"No. Was that why you are following me?"

Eritha shook her head. "It's because I couldn't wait until you contacted me. I guessed you would go to Manex tonight. I've got the information you need. I overheard Alani. I know where Balog is. I can take you there."

CHAPTER 13

The Jedi still kept watch over Manex, who had now retired to his reception room for a rest. Mace covered the front of the residence while Bant stayed outside in the rear. Obi-Wan was positioned behind the curving stairway. From here he had a vantage point to the door of the reception room. He had a feeling it would be a long night.

Use your time. You'll find one day that you have too little of it.

Qui-Gon's words rose in his mind. Obi-Wan was still going over and over what he should have done when he saw his Master. The cloudy aura he felt around Qui-Gon had worried him deeply. He sensed confusion and static, and it prevented him from truly connecting. It had shaken him. Maybe it had prevented him from acting more quickly. Should he have followed

Qui-Gon, gone with him no matter what he said?

Use your time . . .

Obi-Wan didn't think he could. His thoughts were too confused.

That is the time you need discipline most. That is what your training is for.

All right, then. He would stop the voice of Qui-Gon in his head by obeying him.

Although he was tired, although he felt that he had gone over the events of the past days too many times to count, Obi-Wan focused his mind and started again. He went over every event since he and Qui-Gon had stepped foot on New Apsolon. He turned things over in his thoughts, searching for inconsistencies. He considered every unanswered question and every possible answer.

Irini had sworn that she wasn't the one who had fired on them on their first day. They had never discovered who it had been for sure. Balog? They hadn't yet been a threat to him, had they?

Was it just a coincidence that security showed up at Mota's while they were buying the probe droids? It seemed likely now that Alani had told them about Mota in order to trap them. She could have been the one to alert security that the Jedi were buying illegal goods.

The droids must have been reprogrammed to attack Pleni.

Obi-Wan pushed these questions aside. He did not think they would bring him closer to Balog. If only the answers were clear. If only they could get a solid lead. If only Eritha had come through with information on Balog. She had been at her sister's side for more than two days now. Surely she must have learned something.

Would it prove too difficult for Eritha to betray her sister?

But she had already taken a step she could not retake, Obi-Wan knew. On finding out that her sister was behind Tahl's kidnapping, she had gone in search of Obi-Wan and Qui-Gon. She had risked much to do so. She could easily have lost her life in the cave. Obi-Wan remembered how afraid Eritha had been as the explosives were going off and the cave was collapsing. He admired how she'd been able to go on so bravely despite her fear. He still remembered her scream. *They forgot me! They left without me!*

Obi-Wan concentrated for a moment. There was something about the way Eritha had sounded that bothered him now. What was it? The emotion that was driving her was slightly off from what he would expect.

Astonished. She'd been astonished. And betrayed.

They forgot me!

As if they shouldn't have, as if she were somehow privileged, even though she was a prisoner.

If she had been a prisoner . . .

And why had she been heading toward the *back* of the cave?

Yes, the smoke had been thick near the front of the cave. But wouldn't she have tried to push through?

She was heading for the other exit near the back of the cave, Obi-Wan realized. But how had she known about it? They had not found it when Eritha had been captured. She should have had no way of knowing how deep the cave was.

Slow down, Obi-Wan warned himself. There could be other explanations for what had happened. Eritha had been panicked. She was reacting, not thinking.

But since the suspicion had been lodged in his mind, Obi-Wan went back to Eritha's behavior while they were together. He concentrated, bringing the memory back moment by moment, as fresh as if it had happened that morning.

Eritha had seemed sincere when she caught

up with them. Shortly after, they'd been attacked by the Rock Workers. Eritha had been genuinely surprised by the attack, Obi-Wan was sure, and genuinely afraid. When Qui-Gon had warned her to stay behind them, she had readily agreed.

So why then did she suddenly dodge forward when their probe droid was in sight? She had forced them to protect her. As a result, Obi-Wan had received a leg injury and their probe droid had been destroyed. Could it have been a desperate attempt to destroy their only method of tracking Balog?

And what about the attack on the Rock Worker settlement? Qui-Gon had told him that he had met up with Eritha before dawn. She had been planning to refuel the speeders. Or so she had said. But what if she'd actually been planning to leave? If she and Alani were plotting against the Jedi, they had done their work. Qui-Gon and Obi-Wan were without a probe droid. They had no way to track Balog. Eritha had not known that Obi-Wan was better and was able to travel. She would have most likely assumed that Qui-Gon would stay in the settlement.

Maybe she was leaving because she knew of the attack.

Could it be possible? Obi-Wan wondered.

Could Eritha have misled them into thinking that she was the good sister? Were both sisters out for the power they could grab?

There was one last thing. When Obi-Wan and Eritha had arrived back in New Apsolon, Eritha had been furious that Manex had stepped in and offered his own med team for Tahl. Obi-Wan had seen it in her eyes. He had thought it was because she held the same distrust for Manex as he did and was concerned about Tahl's recovery. But what if the opposite were true? What if she *didn't* want Tahl to recover?

What if he had suspected the wrong person? What if Manex was good, and Eritha was bad? Never had he longed for Qui-Gon more.

When Manex had told them of his decision to run for office, Obi-Wan had brought up Alani. Why had Manex hesitated? Was there a reason he was running against Ewane's daughter?

Obi-Wan rubbed his eyes. The lack of sleep and rest was getting to him. His thoughts whirled. He didn't know if he was constructing a case against Eritha on no evidence, or whether this was worth pursuing. Why would the twins call for Tahl's help in the first place, if they planned a power grab all along? It didn't make sense.

Obi-Wan knew his mind would not rest until he had found out some answers. He went to the door of Manex's reception room and pressed the indicator light that would alert Manex that he had a visitor.

The door hissed open a few seconds later. "Is it Balog?" Manex whispered from the darkness.

"No. I need to ask you some questions," Obi-Wan said, stepping inside.

Manex powered up a low light by his sleep couch. He swung his legs over and rubbed his eyes. "I am at your service."

"Why did you insist on your own med team for Tahl?" Obi-Wan asked bluntly. "Surely the team for the Supreme Governor is just as good."

"But mine is better," Manex said. "Don't you remember that I have the best of everything?" He tried to say this jokingly, but it sounded hollow.

"Is there some reason you don't trust Alani and Eritha?" Obi-Wan asked. "If so, you must tell the truth. If you have a suspicion, you must name it."

Manex looked away for a moment, thinking. "I have no real proof," he said slowly. "I did not think it fair to speak until I had some evidence. Those girls have been through so much. First the death of their father, then their protector. At first I thought I was crazy to suspect them."

"Suspect them of what?" Obi-Wan demanded.

"Of working with the Absolutes," Manex told him. "A terrible accusation for the daughters of a Worker hero. But that is why I am running for Supreme Governor against Alani. I can't watch the government fall into the hands of the corrupt again."

"What makes you suspect them? And are you sure it is both of them?"

"Alani does not make a move without Eritha," Manex said. "And Eritha does not make a move without Alani. As I said, I have no proof. Just a couple of overheard words. Unguarded moments. The way they communicate to each other. I sensed a falseness in their grieving for Roan. And today, when I heard that Qui-Gon had been in the United Legislature, I also found out one thing — he had been with Eritha just before the security squad was sent after him."

"Do you think she turned him in?"

"I don't know," Manex said. He spread his hands. "I'm sorry. It isn't much to go on. You see why I didn't want to say anything. I know nothing for sure. It is all instinct."

"I believe in instinct," Obi-Wan said, and headed for the door.

He took the back exit of the dwelling. He didn't want to run into Mace. Bant came forward out of the shadows as he hurried across the lawn.

"Obi-Wan, where are you going?"

"Tell Mace I need to talk to Eritha," Obi-Wan said.

"But can't it wait?" Bant asked, frowning.

"No. Nothing can wait. I'll explain later. Tell Mace that I'm gone." Obi-Wan did not think that Balog would attack tonight, but he knew Mace and Bant could handle it if it happened. He was more worried about Qui-Gon. Qui-Gon still trusted Eritha.

The Supreme Governor's residence was close by. Obi-Wan circled around the building to the back. If he remembered the layout correctly, Eritha's room was at the back. She had no reason to think that Obi-Wan suspected her. She would join him outside, and then he could question her. If he had the slightest feeling that his doubts about her were correct, he would demand that Mace let him find Qui-Gon.

When he reached the back area, he saw that someone was walking along the dark lawn. At first he didn't know which twin it was. But as she came forward, he knew for certain it was Alani. The two girls were almost identical. Perhaps they could fool others. They were not able to fool him.

"Good evening, Alani," he said.

"I see you couldn't sleep, either," Alani said. "Tomorrow is a big day. My name is being presented to the people for the vote. I'll fulfill my father's legacy."

Obi-Wan decided on the spot to be bold. He would not get anywhere playing games with Alani. "Your father's legacy?" he asked. "But Ewane was never in league with the Absolutes. They just imprisoned and tortured him. You have changed his legacy, I think."

Alani looked deeply shocked for just a moment. Then she forced out a laugh. "You're joking."

"No. I'm making a point." Obi-Wan took another step toward her. "I believe you are nothing like your father."

Alani took an involuntary step back. Then she gathered her courage and raised her chin. "It doesn't matter what you think. Eritha told me that we have nothing to fear from the Jedi any longer. Your friend is chasing air. Soon you'll be too busy trying to get him out of jail. And I will rule New Apsolon."

"Are you so sure of yourself?" Obi-Wan asked. "Are you so sure you won't be exposed?"

"Exposure is no longer possible," Alani said. "The Jedi have no proof. The people of New Apsolon love me. Eritha was right."

"So Eritha is your ally."

"She is my sister and my protector. She is part of me," Alani said. "She told me that she was smarter than the Jedi, and she was right. She told me not to worry. I can rule New Apsolon with her by my side. Eritha doesn't like the limelight, but she wants the power. I like it when people are around me and want to talk to me. So I will rule, and she will tell me what to do the way she always has. She told me she would take care of Qui-Gon, and she is doing just that. It was so simple a child could do it. And we are not children anymore. We never had a childhood. Our mother died. Our father was imprisoned. Then he became ruler, and we never saw him. So we can take the only thing he left us, his good name, and make something of ourselves. That's what Eritha says."

He had to keep her talking. Alani, he saw, was not as clever as Eritha.

"What about Tahl?" he asked, ignoring the surge of anger that rocked him when he mentioned her name. The anger would flow through him and pass. "She was kind to you and you betrayed her."

"She was useful," Alani said, coloring for a moment. "I didn't think she would die. But Eritha says that she will be useful again. Because of Tahl, Qui-Gon will trust Eritha without thinking. He will go with her wherever she wants, even to World Security headquarters itself. That is how smart my sister is. She planted a tracking device on Qui-Gon today at the Legislature. We've known where he is at all times. She will lead him right to security headquarters, and he will follow her! If he escapes, it doesn't matter. They'll find him anyway. Isn't that a clever plan?"

It was all he needed. Without another word, Obi-Wan whirled and ran.

"You're too late, Obi-Wan!" Alani shouted after him. "Just like you were too late for Tahl!"

CHAPTER 14

Obi-Wan raced down the wide boulevard, heading for the government buildings. He fervently hoped he wasn't too late.

The World Security headquarters loomed ahead, a squat gray building. He saw two figures hurrying toward it. On one side of the building was a large pen that held hovercraft and swoops. On the other side was the high stone wall that separated the parkland from the road.

"Qui-Gon!" he shouted.

Qui-Gon turned and saw him. Eritha touched his arm, obviously urging him to ignore Obi-Wan and enter the building. Obi-Wan put on a burst of speed and reached out to the Force. He leaped.

At the top of his leap, the doors to the security headquarters flew open. Officers and attack droids spilled down the stairs.

The Force must have warned Qui-Gon, for his

lightsaber was activated and in his hand before Obi-Wan hit the ground near him. With one hand, Qui-Gon pushed Eritha out of the danger and leaped forward to cover her.

By now Obi-Wan was close enough to speak to Qui-Gon. "They won't harm her. She betrayed you," he said, taking up his position next to Qui-Gon.

Qui-Gon didn't react. He kept his eyes on the officers and droids, which were wheeling in formation in front.

"We must take out the droids," Qui-Gon told him. "Don't harm an officer. I'm wanted. They're only doing their job. As soon as the last attack droid goes down, we leave. What do you say we take the offensive?"

Qui-Gon and Obi-Wan leaped together in one motion. The droids began to pepper them with blaster fire. The security officers stayed behind durablast shields, waiting for the droids to do their work.

The Jedi's lightsabers moved in tandem, blocking blaster fire and sending it zinging back in the droids' direction. The security officers ducked behind their shields at the surprising return of fire.

The droids fanned out in a flanking maneuver. Obi-Wan and Qui-Gon split up. Obi-Wan took the left, Qui-Gon the right. One by one, they smashed their way through the line.

Initially, the officers kept behind their shields. But as the battle waned and the blaster fire petered out, they grew more bold. Some drew their blasters and fired.

"Now, Padawan!" Qui-Gon shouted, deflecting fire.

The two Jedi leaped over a line of security vehicles. Blaster fire ripped into the vehicles a split second later. With another great leap, Obi-Wan and Qui-Gon landed on the other side of the park wall. Obi-Wan had just enough time to see Eritha's twisted look of rage as they reached safety. That told him everything he needed to know.

They took off through the darkness of the park. Obi-Wan heard the distant sound of a revving hoverscout.

"Master, Eritha planted a tracking device on you somehow," Obi-Wan said. "At the Legislature today."

"When she embraced me," Qui-Gon said. As he ran, he carefully felt his clothing and skin. He found the whisper-light device on the back of his utility belt. He threw it away into the darkness, then veered off in the opposite direction.

The bright lights of the hoverscout swept the

park, but it turned toward the tracking device. Now they could hear security officers crashing through the trees. The attackers would follow the device for a time.

The Jedi kept under the cover of giant trees with leaves that offered a degree of protection. The trees were planted so close together that even swoops would have a hard time maneuvering through them.

Qui-Gon led them along a zigzagging path through the park, ducking when he saw lights overhead and then moving on. He seemed to know the park well, Obi-Wan noted. Soon they were close to the other end of the park. They leaped over the wall and hurried down the dark streets. After a few blocks Obi-Wan recognized where he was. Qui-Gon had brought them to the Worker Sector.

They paused to catch their breath in the shadow of an alley between two tall buildings.

"Thank you, Padawan," Qui-Gon said. "I did not think I needed help. Obviously, I did. How did you know that Eritha would betray me?"

"Instinct," Obi-Wan said. "Alani confirmed it. They are not afraid of anything, let alone the Jedi. Alani said that they no longer feared exposure."

"That must mean they are in possession of

the list," Qui-Gon mused. "So we can stop chasing it."

"Alani gave the impression that Balog is not the killer of Oleg and Pleni," Obi-Wan said. "She said you were chasing air."

"But I saw him right before Oleg was killed," Qui-Gon said.

"Maybe he wasn't after Oleg. Maybe he was after you," Obi-Wan pointed out.

"That is possible," Qui-Gon said slowly.

"Where to next?" Obi-Wan asked. He hoped his Master would allow him to stay by his side. He had already decided that if Qui-Gon told him he must return to Mace, he would not go.

"Mota," Qui-Gon said. "He holds the key."

Qui-Gon activated the laser pointer to indicate to Mota that he had visitors outside. It seemed a long time before the door slid open. Mota stood in the doorway.

"I'm closed," he said. "Even I need my rest. Come back tomorrow."

Holding out a hand, Qui-Gon used the Force to keep the door open. Mota stared at the door, then at Qui-Gon. He shrugged.

"On the other hand, why should I turn down business?" he asked. He turned and disappeared into the warehouse.

The Jedi followed him. They knew the way down the ramp to the lower levels where Mota kept his stash of black-market items.

Mota was waiting. Instead of the Worker unisuit he had worn to do business, he was now dressed in a sleep tunic, his white legs thrust into a threadbare pair of slippers.

"What is it this time, Jedi? Another probe droid? Did you lose another one? You have the worst luck of anyone I've ever met."

"We want information," Qui-Gon said.

Mota eyed him. "Information has a price, too."

Obi-Wan saw his Master's frustration boil over. He had never seen Qui-Gon this angry before.

"The price will be that I do not break apart every item in this warehouse," Qui-Gon said, taking a step toward Mota.

The man suddenly looked frail in his nightshirt next to Qui-Gon's size and strength. "N-now, relax, we're all friends here," he stuttered.

"I'm not your friend, and I'm not here to relax!" Qui-Gon thundered. "I'm here to find out why my droids were reprogrammed. And you have the answer."

Mota backed up until a table was between him and Qui-Gon.

"I'm not sure what you mean," he said.

Obi-Wan spoke quickly, wanting to give Qui-Gon a moment to control his anger. *If* he could control it. Obi-Wan's worry increased. This was a Qui-Gon he had never seen. Qui-Gon's sense of urgency had always been controlled. If anger came, it came in flashes of lightning that left serenity behind.

"We know that the probe droids were reprogrammed, Mota," Obi-Wan said in a calmer tone. "They never went after Balog at all. Instead they attacked two other beings. The question is, did you do it?"

Mota swallowed. "It wasn't me," he said quickly. "I don't know who it was. Someone broke into my files. I have a warning system built in, so I knew the next time I accessed them."

"When?" Qui-Gon asked.

"Within hours after you left," Mota said. "I don't know how. Or who. You can't trust anyone these days."

"How did the security forces know that Qui-Gon had bought those droids?" Obi-Wan asked.

"They asked me," Mota said in a small voice. "All my droids are coded. They tracked the droids here. I told them the Jedi Qui-Gon had bought them. I had to tell the truth. You wouldn't want me to land in jail, would you?" Mota tried to smile.

Qui-Gon gave him an even stare. Mota backed up even farther. "Ah, I guess I should have mentioned to the officers that I suspected the droids were reprogrammed. But when speaking to security officers, it's better not to answer questions they don't ask. They might have gone through all my files. I wouldn't be able to protect my clients. And I would be out of business. Nobody wants that. You might need another probe droid, for example —"

"We need access to your computers," Obi-Wan said brusquely. "Right now."

"Of course, help yourself." Mota hurriedly pointed to his datascreen. "Just don't erase any profits, heh heh."

Qui-Gon immediately began clicking keys and accessing datafiles. "Did you try to trace the break-in?"

"No," Mota admitted. "I'm not that advanced. I just know how to track inventory and money."

Qui-Gon continued to move through Mota's files with astonishing speed. Obi-Wan knew he was missing nothing. He could see the level of concentration on his Master's face.

Qui-Gon hit a few keys, activating a search mode Obi-Wan didn't recognize. Within seconds, he got a reply.

"Do you recognize this code?" he asked, pointing to the datascreen.

Mota leaned closer. "It's the Worker data address," he said. "It's already in my files."

"Who uses it?" Qui-Gon asked.

Mota's face was tinged blue from the datascreen. "Irini and Lenz," he said.

CHAPTER 15

Obi-Wan dashed after Qui-Gon. His Master had moved so quickly he had not had time to gather his thoughts or decide on a direction. He had expected him to head for the ramp to the street, but instead Qui-Gon ran to the lower level. He needed fast transport.

"Open those bay doors!" Qui-Gon yelled to Mota as he ran.

Unease thudded with every heartbeat as Obi-Wan chased after Qui-Gon. He had never seen his Master like this. Qui-Gon seemed to barely register his surroundings or Obi-Wan's presence. All his will was directed at his goal.

It was the goal that worried Obi-Wan. Was it justice . . . or revenge?

By the time they reached the lower level, the door at the end of the long warehouse space stood open. Qui-Gon jumped into an airspeeder. Obi-Wan barely had time to scramble into the passenger seat when Qui-Gon throttled the engines and zoomed down the tunnel.

The engines were pushed almost to full, much too fast to maneuver in the tunnel. Obi-Wan could see that the bay doors at the end of the tunnel had not had a chance to open. Still Qui-Gon did not reduce his speed.

Obi-Wan whipped his head around to face him. Qui-Gon wasn't just pressing his luck. This was pure recklessness. "Master!"

Qui-Gon's face seemed carved from the gray stone of New Apsolon. His lips were a thin line. His hands stayed steady on the controls. He seemed not to hear Obi-Wan.

A crack of gray light appeared ahead. It widened. The doors were opening, but too slowly for Obi-Wan's comfort.

"Hang on!" Qui-Gon warned.

Obi-Wan just had time to clutch for support as Qui-Gon flipped the airspeeder sideways. Without slackening speed, he zoomed through the opening, clearing it by centimeters. They flew into the dark night.

Obi-Wan pressed himself back into the seat, trying to still his ragged breathing. Qui-Gon seemed poised on the brink of losing control. There didn't seem anything Obi-Wan could do or say to stop him or get him to slow down. Obi-Wan tried to stifle his own panic. He had to trust his Master.

But for the first time in their long partnership, he didn't think he could. That knowledge made fear grasp him by the throat.

Qui-Gon piloted the craft expertly through the deserted streets. He pulled up in front of Lenz's hideout and flew up the stairs. He pounded on Lenz's door. They heard the creak of a floor-board.

"Don't try your escape route," Qui-Gon warned. "We'll find you."

The door opened. Lenz looked at them warily. He looked more frail than usual, his skin pale and shiny. "It's the middle of the night."

Qui-Gon slammed the door open wider and strode inside. "I need to speak with you and Irini. If she's not here, contact her."

"She is here. But you can't see her," Lenz said quietly. "She's ill —"

Qui-Gon ignored him and pulled open a closed door. He stopped short. Obi-Wan came up behind him. Irini lay on a sleep couch, covered in a blanket. She was shivering, and her face shone with sweat.

"What is it? What's wrong?" Obi-Wan asked.

Lenz pushed past him to kneel by Irini's side. "A blaster attack. She won't see a medic."

Obi-Wan hurried forward. "She needs bacta."

"I know," Lenz said.

"Who did this?" Qui-Gon demanded.

"Balog," Irini said through clenched teeth. "He has the list now."

"So you had the list all along?" Qui-Gon asked her.

"No. I stole it from Legislator Pleni."

Obi-Wan glanced at Qui-Gon. Did that mean that Irini had reprogrammed the droids to attack the Legislator? Was she a murderer?

She saw the look that passed between them. "I . . . had to get . . . that list," she said, in obvious pain. "I didn't want anyone to die. But I couldn't let anyone stand in my way, either."

"And you wanted me to get blamed for it?" Qui-Gon asked.

She shook her head. "I was surprised at that. But I could hardly come forward to clear you."

Qui-Gon bent down and swiftly examined Irini's wounds. His anger seemed to have drained away at the sight of her distress. She needed help. "Your wounds won't kill you if you see a medic. But I see signs of infection already."

"That's what I told her," Lenz said. He brushed back damp hair from Irini's forehead. "She still refuses."

"Did you send your probe droids after Oleg, too?" Obi-Wan asked.

Irini nodded. "I was tracking him. I told Qui-Gon I wanted to protect Oleg, but it was a lie. He betrayed us. We needed the list. If he had only given it up . . . if Pleni had only given it up . . . none of this would have happened."

"Why?" Obi-Wan asked. "You said you had renounced violence."

Irini pressed her lips together and did not answer.

"She did it for me," Lenz said.

"Lenz —" Irini began warningly.

"It has gone too far, Irini." Lenz's voice was tender. "You have protected me too long. Do you think I will watch you die for me, too?" He turned to the Jedi. "My name is on the list."

"You were an informer?" Qui-Gon asked.

"He was tortured," Irini said. She let out a small gasp and closed her eyes in pain. "What they did to him . . . no one should have to endure."

"That is not an excuse," Lenz said firmly. "I confessed to Irini, and she forgave me. Others would not. I gave the Absolutes information —"

Irini struggled to sit up, but the pain made her lie flat again. "Don't tell them, Lenz," she begged. "It is our secret. It can remain our secret. Your career is too important. You are a great leader —"

"No," Lenz said sadly. "I am no longer, if I ever was. The Workers will go on without me." He turned to the Jedi. "This was five years ago. The Absolutes raided a meeting place. Two Workers were killed, the rest imprisoned. They let me go." He looked at Irini sadly. "Now we both have two deaths on our conscience, Irini."

He stood. "I am going to call a med team." Irini protested, but Lenz went on firmly. "Balog has the list now. He has won. He will remove his own name from the list, and all the secrets will be revealed. He will discredit his enemies, including me." Lenz looked tenderly at Irini. "As for my Irini, I would rather have her alive and imprisoned than dead."

Irini turned her face to the wall. Obi-Wan saw her shoulders shake with sobs.

Lenz turned to the Jedi. "I did not know what Irini had done, and I'm sorry to hear that you were blamed for her crimes. We owe you our help now more than ever. You know that Alani is running for Supreme Governor. Recently we have realized that though she wants Worker support, she does not need it. Someone else is supporting her — with finances that we do not have. This has made us suspicious. I have received news tonight from our spy in the Supreme Governor's residence. He's discovered that there is a secret tunnel between the residence and the Absolute Museum. In the old days it was used when those captured were secretly transported to Absolute headquarters. The museum is closed now. It is just a guess, but wouldn't it be the perfect place for Balog and the Absolutes to hide? The twins could smuggle him in and out easily until Alani is elected tomorrow."

It made sense, Obi-Wan realized. It would be like Balog to hide in the one place so obvious that they would never think to look there, the site of the recording of the great wrongs the Absolutes had visited on New Apsolon.

By the look on his Master's face, Obi-Wan

could tell that Qui-Gon had reached the same conclusion.

"We must go tonight," Qui-Gon said. "Tomorrow will be too late."

CHAPTER 16

They sped through the dark, empty streets back to the Civilized Sector. Obi-Wan knew that Qui-Gon felt that Balog was in their grasp. And right now Qui-Gon was giving every sign of a man bent on revenge.

He was almost afraid to say anything. The look on Qui-Gon's face was so forbidding. The years of experience with his Master, the closeness they'd shared, it all seemed to evaporate in the night air. Qui-Gon was like a stranger.

He had thought that if only he could be with his Master, he would be able to help him control his ravaged feelings of grief and anger. He had spent the past days in torment, thinking that he needed to be by Qui-Gon's side. Now he saw that his presence had no meaning for Qui-Gon. His Master was lost in his own quest. If he was bent on revenge, Obi-Wan might not be able to interfere. Qui-Gon's will combined with his great skills might make him impossible to stop. Obi-Wan felt chilled at the thought. He would have to try.

Tonight he could lose his Master to the dark path. The impossible had become possible. He could feel it in the dark energy within the Force, swirling and crashing around Qui-Gon. Never had he felt so helpless.

Obi-Wan gathered his own connection to the Force. He resolved that no matter what, he would remain by his Master's side. He could not lose hope. He would protect his Master from himself if he had to. He would not lose Qui-Gon on this dark night.

Qui-Gon pulled up in front of the Supreme Governor's residence.

"Master, we should contact Mace Windu," Obi-Wan said.

Qui-Gon leaped out of the speeder. "Whatever you want."

Obi-Wan activated his comlink as he jumped out of the speeder and ran after Qui-Gon. He spoke hastily into the comlink to Mace about what they had learned.

"Wait for us," Mace said. "We're close."

"It's too late," Obi-Wan said, as Qui-Gon began cutting a hole in the front door of the residence with his lightsaber.

He shut off the comlink and followed Qui-Gon

through the hole. The security devices sounded an alarm, and a security officer emerged from the booth. He eyed the Jedi but did not draw his blaster.

"Lenz called ahead," he said. "I'll shut these down. I already disabled the link to World Security."

Qui-Gon nodded. Obi-Wan was glad for this bit of luck. The Workers' spy was on duty. Of course the twins had heard the commotion, but at least security reinforcements wouldn't be called. They would only have to deal with the security in the residence itself, at least for a time.

Lenz had given them details on how to reach the tunnel. Qui-Gon ran toward the back of the house, Obi-Wan matching his stride. They knew the entrance was in a storage area for the kitchens.

They burst into the storage area. Eritha stood casually in the middle of the floor, holding two blasters aimed at their chests.

"You have to kill me to get through that door," she said. She looked older than her years. Her face was pale, and her eyes glittered. Her gold hair straggled down her back.

"I am prepared to do that," Qui-Gon said.

Obi-Wan did not glance at his Master. He hoped Qui-Gon was bluffing. He did not know how close to the edge Qui-Gon was. He couldn't sense his Master any longer. There was only grayness and static between them.

"You think I will not attack because you are a young girl," Qui-Gon said. "But the moment you set out on your path to power, you took on the consequences of an adult. You are responsible for Tahl's death."

"I am not responsible!" Eritha said shrilly. "Others have survived the sensory deprivation device. Why couldn't she? She was a Jedi!"

"She was locked in it for days," Qui-Gon said. "Far longer than any Absolute prisoner."

He spoke in a flat, unemotional tone. Somehow he had pushed grief down so far that it did not tinge his words. That worried Obi-Wan more than his earlier display of anger. Did this mean that Qui-Gon had now accepted his revenge and was willing and ready to act on it?

"I didn't have anything against Tahl," Eritha said. "She is a casualty of war. We brought her here because we knew she would come. Everything was all planned. We needed a Jedi presence at first to cover for us. With Jedi support the rest would be easy. Balog would kidnap us and Roan would resign. Alani would run for his post. Then we found out about the list. Balog was on it. We knew Roan had it, and we knew he was waiting to expose Balog. He thought Balog had been his friend. He didn't want to expose him, but he would. Everyone would know that Balog had been an Absolute. It would have spoiled our plans! We had to get that list. You'd think as head of World Security that Balog would be helpful. He was useless. He leaked the information to the Absolutes, and someone stole the list. Only he didn't bring it to Balog. He kept it so he could sell it. We didn't know who it was."

"Oleg," Obi-Wan said. He wanted to keep Eritha talking. He was uneasy about how Qui-Gon's urgency had changed to a deadly calm. He could feel through the Force that there was no serenity in this calm. Qui-Gon was staring at Eritha as though she were an obstacle, not a person.

"Yes. Just our luck — the Absolute who gets his hands on the list turns out to be a Worker spy," Eritha said. "But all we knew then was that someone had it. We needed help — more help than Balog could give us. We needed someone with brains and courage. It was lucky that Tahl was coming. I knew we could get her to help us without knowing it. She was generous that way. She would do what we asked. She still thought of us as helpless young girls with no mother or real father."

Qui-Gon closed his eyes.

"We let her think it was her idea to infiltrate

the Absolutes. We knew she'd find out about the list and try to get it for us."

"She trusted you," Obi-Wan said.

Eritha shrugged. "Everyone trusts us. That's our advantage. We are the daughters of the great hero Ewane. The great hero who barely spent one day in his daughters' presence but passed them off to strangers to raise. The great hero who only thought about his planet, not his own flesh and blood." Eritha's lip curled. "Why shouldn't we use that trust? Tahl did everything we asked and more. When she was seen escaping with Oleg, we thought she had the list. But she didn't bring it to us, so we had to take it. Everything was completely logical. If Tahl had only told us the truth — that she didn't have the list — she wouldn't be dead."

"Balog would have killed her anyway," Obi-Wan said.

"You don't know that," Eritha said craftily. "He might have let her go."

"You're lying," Qui-Gon said flatly.

"Maybe." Obi-Wan was shocked at the cruelty in Eritha's eyes, like a large creature playing with a tiny one before gobbling it up. "You'll never know. Maybe it's your fault that Tahl is dead, Qui-Gon."

Obi-Wan saw the color drain from Qui-Gon's face. He saw his hand move toward his lightsaber. Obi-Wan could wait no longer. He threw himself forward at Eritha, who had locked eyes with Qui-Gon, taunting him.

His leg shot out, knocking one blaster from her hand. She screamed but he was already twisting behind her, grabbing her other wrist and wrenching the blaster from it. He tucked both in his belt.

"You hurt me!" she cried, grabbing her wrist.

"Qui-Gon, hurry," Obi-Wan urged. His Master hadn't moved. But at his words he rushed forward toward the tunnel entrance.

"You killed her, Qui-Gon!" Eritha screamed after them as they accessed the tunnel door. "Live with that, if you live at all!"

CHAPTER 17

Qui-Gon had no doubt that within minutes Eritha would send security attack droids after them. He knew that ahead of them, the Absolutes would be well armed. He gave no more thought to the obstacles than to a pesky insect. He did not strategize. He would charge ahead, and he would win. That was all he knew.

Qui-Gon saw Obi-Wan give a quick glance at him. He told himself not to display the temper he had showed at Mota's. His Padawan was worried about how quick to anger he was. Qui-Gon himself had been surprised at how his anger had continued to rise. He knew he was feeding it instead of letting it go. It gave him speed and focus.

He knew his attitude was bringing him dangerously close to the dark side. He knew with a chance for silence and stillness he would be able to see this. But he didn't have the luxury.

He would have to count on his own ability to control his anger at the proper time.

The tunnel ran below the governor's residence. It had been unused for many years, and was dark and stuffy. Qui-Gon ran by the light of his saber. He knew Obi-Wan was behind him. His Padawan would give him support, but he knew he did not need it. This was between him and Balog.

Eritha's words had stunned him, but he had filed them away for the long sleepless nights ahead of him. Balog was his object.

The tunnel ended in a durasteel door. Qui-Gon cut through it and stepped inside. He was in the lower level of the museum.

"Droids behind us, Qui-Gon," Obi-Wan spoke quietly in his ear. "Coming from the residence."

A nuisance. They would have to be dealt with before they could proceed.

Qui-Gon turned as the first droids tumbled through the opening, already engaging them in blaster fire. They were lucky. The droids were programmed to advance, but they were not programmed to strategize. They simply took the easiest route to their prey and poured through the opening in the door, where Qui-Gon and Obi-Wan were waiting.

Obi-Wan deflected fire while slicing at the droids. Impatiently, Qui-Gon swung his lightsaber like a club. He had no time for finesse. He needed to cut down as many droids as possible in the shortest amount of time.

Obi-Wan was a blur by his side. Qui-Gon was grateful for his Padawan's speed. Soon the floor was littered with smoking droids.

There were only two more left. "Take them down," Qui-Gon told Obi-Wan, and raced away.

It was lucky that he and Obi-Wan had taken the tour of the museum upon their arrival on New Apsolon. He could remember each level and room. This level was used for storage, so they hadn't toured it. The floors and walls were bare and damp. On the floor overhead were the cells and torture rooms, as well as the offices. No doubt the Absolutes were camped there. Including Balog.

Qui-Gon accessed the turbolift to the next level. He strode out into the hall. He saw a figure ahead. It was a man dressed in a navy tunic. An Absolute. He froze when he saw Qui-Gon. Then he doubled back and ran the way he had come.

Qui-Gon chased after him. No doubt he had gone to spread an alarm. The Absolutes weren't expecting invaders, but they would meet them with resistance.

He burst into the room just as the Absolute activated a row of attack droids that had been on display. To Qui-Gon's surprise, the attack droids immediately lined up. They were operational. The Absolutes had armed the displays in the museum.

This was more sophisticated weaponry than Eritha's droids. Blaster fire was erratic and came from the droids' chests, foreheads, and hands. They could wheel and maneuver and twist themselves into flexible positions.

Qui-Gon was outnumbered, but he refused to be outmatched. Blaster fire rocketed toward him in a fiery curtain. Every part of him was vulnerable. His lightsaber had to keep pace with the rapid fire as he took evasive action. He had a shock when he realized that he might have to retreat.

He felled two droids, but the others were relentless. Some rushed toward him, blasting fire. The others flanked him and aimed as they tried to get behind him. Qui-Gon felt sweat roll down his forehead, stinging his eyes. He used the Force to smash one against the wall, but it reformed and came after him again. He used his lightsaber to cut it in half.

He had never been happier to see Obi-Wan in his life. His Padawan suddenly leaped into the fray, lightsaber swinging. With Obi-Wan's help, Qui-Gon was able to regroup and smash the two droids to his left. The two Jedi swung wide and came at the droids' line from each end. They each felled two, then leaped toward the center of the line to destroy two more droids as they shifted into position.

Smoke rose, choking them. Obi-Wan took out the last droid, and they stumbled out of the small room.

Obi-Wan leaned over to take a breath of pure air. "Where do you think Balog is?"

The question seemed to echo inside Qui-Gon's brain. He realized that he hadn't given much thought to Balog's whereabouts. He had just charged ahead. That wasn't like him.

I am not thinking clearly, he told himself. *I am reacting, not acting.*

He realized this meant he was on the edge of his control. But even as he recognized this, he recognized something equally chilling: *He did not care.*

And suddenly, he knew where Balog might be. Remembering the tour, he recalled a tech center on this floor. Since Balog had recently stolen the list from Irini, he was most likely accessing it on a datascreen. He would certainly waste no time erasing his name and looking for others to denounce.

Before he could answer Obi-Wan, more droids wheeled around the corner behind them. They felt a warming in the Force before the blaster fire began. Once again, Qui-Gon and Obi-Wan had to use every particle of concentration to defeat the agile droids. The blaster fire seemed to come from everywhere.

The droids were between them and the data center. Rage filled Qui-Gon at the delay. Every second that passed meant that Balog would have a chance to escape.

He charged at the droids, swinging his lightsaber in a constant arc, hardly noticing when blaster fire zinged near his ears or barely missed an arm or hand. He savagely swung at the droids, destroying one after another. Obi-Wan tried to protect him as best he could, but even he could not keep up with the fierceness of Qui-Gon's attack.

Qui-Gon broke through the line of droids, kicking one aside and cleaving it in two. He had always thought that giving in to rage would make him sloppy. Instead, he felt precise. He felt powerful. His rage filled him with purpose.

The droids were defeated, in pieces, smoking around him. He dashed ahead.

"Qui-Gon, wait!"

But he ignored his Padawan. He could not wait.

With this new sharpness of mind, he remembered the exact location of the data room. He did not hesitate but threw open the door. He could hear Obi-Wan only steps behind him, and he felt a stab of disappointment. He wished Obi-Wan had stayed behind.

He wanted to meet Balog alone.

The squat, powerful man sat at a tech console. He spun around in his chair, a look of surprise on his face. So Eritha had not been able to reach him.

Qui-Gon took in the small dark eyes, the small pursed mouth, the round head. He focused his hatred on this man. Here was the man who had watched Tahl's health deteriorate slowly, day by agonizing day, and felt nothing. Here was the man who had not recognized that he was slowly crushing an extraordinary spirit.

This little, evil man.

The injustice of it staggered Qui-Gon. This man was alive. Tahl was dead. His vision blurred at the emotion that roared inside him.

Balog rose, kicking his chair out of his way. He reached for the blaster on his belt.

Qui-Gon smiled.

Obi-Wan stood next to him, his lightsaber held in a defensive stance, waiting for Balog to make the first move.

With one hand, Balog reached over to activate the comm unit on the tech console. "I need help in the data center. Send attack droids —"

With a casual gesture, Qui-Gon buried his

lightsaber in the console. Sparks flew, and smoke curled from the circuits.

Balog fired. Obi-Wan sprang forward to deflect it.

The blaster fire was nothing to Qui-Gon. It was merely a momentary barrier between himself and Balog. Balog was his prey. A collection of skin and muscles and bones that must be brought down in a heap.

His lightsaber moved like a trick of light, so fast that each stroke was a memory. It was so easy to deflect Balog's pathetic fire. Panic rose in Balog's eyes and made him clumsy. He dropped his blaster. He tried to run, but his legs tangled in the chair he had kicked away. He fell with a crash to the floor.

At last, Qui-Gon's enemy lay at his feet, just as he'd imagined. He stood over Balog, his lightsaber high, prepared for the stroke that would bring him so much satisfaction.

"No, Qui-Gon."

The voice seemed to come from far away, yet it was so close to his ear. It confused him.

He turned and met Obi-Wan's eyes. He felt he was seeing him from a great distance. Confusion swept over him.

Then it was as though clouds parted, and clarity came. He saw so much in a moment. In his Padawan's steady glance he saw both fear and compassion.

He was no longer far away. The distance compressed, and he was in the same room with Obi-Wan. Qui-Gon returned to himself, and saw how far he had gone. The dark side had risen in his blood. He had known it and encouraged it. Shaking, he deactivated his lightsaber and tucked it back in his belt.

He had come close to taking a life out of revenge. Only he would know how close. He would never forget it. He would never allow himself to forget it.

Balog closed his eyes in relief. Obi-Wan stood over him and reached for his comlink as Mace and Bant entered the room.

CHAPTER 18

The four Jedi stood on the landing platform high above the city of New Apsolon. Qui-Gon looked down at the stately gray buildings, the curving streets and wide boulevards. From high above it was easy to tell where the grand Civilized Sector began and the smaller, twisting neighborhoods of the Workers ended.

Manex had lent them the finest consular ship on New Apsolon, as well as his personal pilot. Tahl's body had been loaded aboard in a small room fragrant with native flowers. The Jedi would accompany her on her last journey back to the Temple.

They left behind them a government still torn by division. Alani, Eritha, and Balog had been arrested. There had been a huge outcry at the arrest of the twins. Both Workers and many Civilized did not believe they could be corrupt. Not the daughters of Ewane.

Irini was recovering in a med center, but charges had been filed against her. The Worker movement had lost Irini and Lenz in one stroke. They were struggling to find new leaders.

The turbolift doors opened and Manex stepped out. He was dressed in a rich robe of his favorite shade of green. He walked forward and bowed to the Jedi.

"The people of New Apsolon owe you a great debt," he said.

"There is still unrest on New Apsolon," Mace said. "But the government will proceed with honesty."

Manex nodded. "The elections are now set for next week. Other Legislators have stepped forward to run. I know the Absolute movement has been damaged, but it has not disappeared completely. We still have enemies to fight. No doubt there are more troubles ahead as the Committee to Reinstate Justice deals with the list of Absolute informers. But I have committed myself to my world. If I'm elected, I'll take up where Roan left off."

"If you need us again, we will come," Mace told him.

Qui-Gon turned away. *I will not be the one to come,* he thought. He would never return to New Apsolon again.

"We thank you for your transport," Mace said to Manex. "And for all you have done."

Manex's brown eyes were full of sorrow. "I cannot begin to replace what you lost here. I can only promise you my service for the rest of my life, should you need it."

Manex signaled the pilot on board to lower the ramp of the ship. Then, with a final bow, he walked away.

Qui-Gon stood a short distance from the others. He saw Bant move closer to Obi-Wan.

"Is Qui-Gon all right?" she asked in a low, concerned tone.

"I don't know," his Padawan said. "But he will be."

Will I? Qui-Gon wondered with a curious detachment.

Obi-Wan glanced at Bant. "Are we all right?"

Qui-Gon felt that if it were possible for his heart to be touched, it would be, at the warm look in Bant's eyes. He remembered when he and Tahl had been that close.

"Of course," she told Obi-Wan.

He owed Obi-Wan a word, too. He called him over to his side.

"I need to thank you," he told him. "When I stood over Balog with hate in my heart, you saved me. It was the sound of my name that brought me back to myself."

Obi-Wan looked at him, puzzled. "But I didn't speak."

Qui-Gon's heart swelled. It had been Tahl. Of course it had been Tahl. The voice had been so near and yet so far away. It was her voice, soft and warm, a voice he had heard rarely, and a tone, he now realized, she had reserved only for him.

She was still with him. It should have helped him to know that. But instead, fresh agony ripped through him. It was not enough to have her voice in a time of need. He needed her physical presence. He needed her warm and breathing, close enough to touch, near enough to exchange a private smile.

Obi-Wan must have seen something on his face. He placed a hand on Qui-Gon's shoulder. Qui-Gon did not feel the pressure. He did not want to feel his Padawan's touch. He was grateful to Obi-Wan for his compassion. He owed a debt to Mace and Bant for their silent understanding.

Yet he could not stand to be with them.

Qui-Gon turned away from them and strode up the ramp. He would spend the journey back to Coruscant watching over Tahl alone.

He knew one thing: This grief must be borne, and it would not be a load that lessened with time. It would appear and reappear. It would gather and lose strength, and when he thought it was diminishing, it would rise again. It was too big for Jedi acceptance to contain it.

And what does that mean, to be a Jedi and be unable to accept? Qui-Gon wondered. It was a question for another time.

He entered the ship and did not look behind him. He was leaving on New Apsolon the possibility of a different life, a life that he had looked forward to with a joy he did not know existed in the galaxy. He would return to the life he had, a life of solitary service. He did not know where else to go.

He hoped to find satisfaction in that service again someday. That day seemed far away. For now, he headed for the small room where Tahl lay for his last, long good-bye.

FIRST CAME *STAR WARS: EPISODE I*
COMING SOON IS *STAR WARS: EPISODE II*
IN BETWEEN THERE IS...

JEDI QUEST

After a death-defying pilgrimage to a sacred Jedi site, twelve-year-old Anakin Skywalker is sent with his Jedi master, Obi-Wan Kenobi, on a mission to defeat an evil foe. There, Anakin's gifts are tested—and Anakin is tempted by the darker fate that awaits him.

Wherever Books Are Sold

Visit us at www.scholastic.com/titles/starwars

LUCAS BOOKS

■SCHOLASTIC

SJQT14